Torn By Chance

By: Summer N Dawn

OTHER WORKS BY THE AUTHOR

The Reign Trilogy
Reign Reimagined
Red's Revenge
Love's Freedom

Standalone
From Princess to Queen

Stay dark and spread the love!

TRIGGER WARNINGS

IF ANY OF THE FOLLOWING TRIGGERS YOU
PLEASE REFRAIN FROM READING!
YOUR MENTAL AND PHYSICAL HEALTH
COMES FIRST!

<u>*TRIGGERS:*</u>
PREGNANCY
 ATTEMPTED SUICIDE
PAST TRAUMA
DEATH
MURDER
 RAPE
**Remember, your mental and physical health
matter. If any of these things trigger you, please
refrain from reading!**

*Call or Text or Chat the 988 Suicide & Crisis
Lifeline 988. Hours are available 24/7 and the
cost is free OR Text HOME to 741741 to reach a
trained Crisis Counselor through Crisis Text
Line, a global not-for-profit organization. Free,
24/7, confidential.*

DEDICATION

TO SUNSHINE,

 THANK YOU FOR ALWAYS SUPPORTING
MY IDEAS, NO MATTER HOW CRAZY THEY
ARE! YOU'RE MY CHANCE THAT I AM GLAD
I DIDN'T LET SLIP AWAY.

Torn by Chance

Prologue

Tori

I love my job at Kastways.

Each day presents new challenges and opportunities, allowing me to expand my knowledge and skills in ways I never imagined.

Not only do I get to navigate my responsibilities, but I also thrive on the extra learning experiences that come my way.

Through my time here, I've uncovered the power of leveraging my strengths to manage various situations to my advantage.

It's an empowering realization to understand that I deserve love and happiness.

Along this journey, I've also come to terms with my unique preferences, including a slight kink that makes my romantic encounters more exciting.

Reflecting on my experiences, I've become increasingly aware that genuine love is becoming a rare commodity in today's fast-paced world.

The relentless hustle and bustle of everyday life often overshadows our ability to forge deep, meaningful connections with others.

As we race from one obligation to the next, the warmth and intimacy that once defined our relationships seem to evaporate, leaving many of us yearning for heartfelt bonds that are increasingly hard to find.

I've also gained insight into the shadowy world of the not-so-legal Bratva and its intricate dynamics.

While there's a thrill in understanding that world, it's a double-edged sword—a blessing for the experiences I gain and a curse for the dark realities that come with it.

Amidst these complexities, I simply want a chance at love, a genuine opportunity to thrive personally and professionally.

But I often wonder: Why does my chance at love feel like it's perpetually slipping away?

Am I truly that repulsive?

I can't help but wonder if my moment will come or if it will be overshadowed by the intricacies of my work at Kastways.

Will I be left behind or discarded, like something deemed unworthy?

I understand that chances in life can be fleeting, often coming only once in a lifetime.

Yet, I hope that the one opportunity I need might strike unexpectedly, turning everything around.

So, I ask myself: Which chance will be mine? Will I finally embrace the love I crave, or will I endure the heartbreak of being torn apart yet again? Only time will reveal the answers.

Chapter 1

Gulfport, Mississippi, wasn't always my home.

For two vibrant decades, I called the bustling streets of New York City my own.

My name is Toreeanne Sullivan, and I am the proud daughter of Charles and Tamari Sullivan.

Now, at 29 years old, I reflect on my beginnings. I entered this world on a frigid December day, a moment that etched my dislike for the cold deep within me.

Growing up, my parents embodied everything a child could wish for.

My mother, a warm-hearted librarian at my high school, was cherished by all the students.

She had a magical way of making the library feel like a second home, creating a welcoming oasis filled with endless stories and knowledge.

Her passion for books and nurturing spirit left a lasting impression on me and everyone lucky enough to know her.

You could visit the library and get a book recommendation, life lessons, and support.

My dad was a car salesman who worked to ensure his kids had everything they wanted and needed.

No matter what, my parents didn't tell me no unless it was for my good.

I did not have a cell phone until I graduated high school, so I rode to school with my mom daily.

I never took advantage of my parents because I always saw their hard work.

My world was turned upside down 6 years ago.

I woke up at four am to my phone constantly ringing.

I finally picked it up.

"Hello?"

"Hello, am I speaking to Ms. Torianne Sullivan?"

Nobody calls me by my full name anymore.

"Yes, speaking."

"Ma'am, you must come to the hospital as quickly as possible. Both of your parents have been in a major accident. Your father is currently in surgery, and your mother is waiting to be taken to surgery. Then we're hit by an eighteen-wheeler when the driver fell asleep at the wheel. They had to be cut out of their SUV, and only part of the front end was left. Please come quickly. We are doing everything we can."

It was like my worst fear played out.

I threw on my clothes and rushed to the hospital.

A few minutes after arriving at the hospital, the doctor finally entered the room, where I anxiously waited.

His solemn expression told me everything I needed to know before he even spoke.

They are gone—my parents are gone.

A wave of despair crashed over me, leaving me feeling utterly alone in a world that had suddenly become too big and empty.

At that moment, it felt as if every color had drained from my life, leaving nothing but shades of gray.

I never imagined that my heart could be shattered so wholly, not once but twice within the same year.

First, I faced the unimaginable loss of my parents, who had been my pillars of strength and love. And just when I thought I could find solace, my boyfriend of six years decided to walk away.

He decided to sever the ties of our relationship with nothing more than a text message—a stark, impersonal gesture that felt like a dagger to my heart.

The connection we had nurtured and cherished over the years was instantly reduced to mere words on a screen.

I found myself engulfed in a whirlwind of emotions, grappling with the harsh reality of abandonment at a moment when I craved support and understanding the most.

It was as if everything I had ever known that had brought me comfort and stability was suddenly swept away, leaving me adrift in a world that now felt hopelessly shattered and beyond repair.

The echoes of our shared memories haunted me, amplifying my sense of loss and despair.

"We are not meant to be. I am moving. I hope to meet you again later in life. C"

Just three days before my parents' lives were extinguished, I received that haunting message—a chime that echoed in my mind long after it faded.

In that instant, a crushing weight of solitude enveloped me as if the air itself had thickened, leaving me gasping for breath.

There was no confidant to unburden my thoughts to, no comforting shoulder upon which to lean; I found myself ensnared in a web of overwhelming isolation.

As despair coiled around me like a suffocating shroud, I sank deeper into an abyss of darkness, a desolate realm where the flicker of hope was snuffed out completely.

Each passing moment felt like an eternity, drowning me in an ocean of grief and uncertainty.

I would become so consumed by my thoughts that I would forget to eat or sleep.

Instead, I found myself staring blankly into the distance, lost in a daydream for hours at a time, utterly oblivious to the world around me.

It took me months to snap back to reality.

Two years after all that turmoil, I felt an undeniable urge to seek a new beginning.

During a brief trip to the bustling city of Chicago, I encountered Kass, a woman who exuded strength despite the challenges life had thrust upon her.

Kass, whose full name is Kassani Ballentine, holds a prominent place in her world as the revered Ballentine Queen.

Married to the formidable Masimo Ballentine, the Don or Pakhan of the notorious Ballentine Bratva, she is a powerful figure in her own right.

Since the tender age of eighteen months, Kass has faced the challenges of cerebral palsy, a condition that arose from the devastating effects of Shaken Baby Syndrome.

Her journey through life has been laden with hurdles, both physical and social, shaping her into a remarkable individual.

Kass walks with a distinct limp, a result of uneven muscle development affecting her right side.

This characteristic does not define her; rather, it highlights her incredible resilience and determination. Each step she takes is a testament to her strength and tenacity.

In addition to her physical challenges, Kass sometimes experiences difficulties with her speech, and her words occasionally emerge in a stutter.

This is a poignant reminder of the numerous battles her brain has endured throughout the years.

Yet, despite these obstacles, Kass continues to navigate life with an indomitable spirit that inspires everyone around her.

Despite these challenges, Kass has consistently defied the judgments of those around her and triumphed over her health struggles.

Her life story is not one of fairy-tale perfection but rather a testament to courage and perseverance.

Through every hurdle, she has discovered a profound sense of belonging in a world that often relegates individuals with disabilities to the sidelines.

Kass embodies the spirit of resilience, transforming the narrative of being "handicapped" into one of empowerment and capability.

Her journey has redefined being handicapped, inspiring everyone fortunate enough to cross her path.

Kass and I met at a nail salon.

I was getting a pedicure, and she came in with Asia.

Let's not skip over the fact that Asia is a badass, too.

Asia is the foremost female spy for the Ballentine Bratva, who happens to find love with a fellow Bratva member.

Kass always gives off those motherly vibes; she's the easiest person to talk to.

The three of us became fast friends.

As we chatted over champagne, she excitedly shared her vision of opening a vibrant club in Gulfport, Mississippi.

My future felt uncertain at that moment, and I had no clear direction.

With a spark in her eyes, she said she was looking for a head bartender.

I responded enthusiastically, saying, "If you're willing to teach me, I know I can learn anything."

Little did I know that conversation would be the turning point that set the course for my journey.

The rest, as they say, is history.

Kass' club has been open for almost 3 years.

Does the idea of working for the Bratva intimidate me?

Not in the slightest.

I've already endured the pain of losing everything that once held immense value in my life.

The thought of facing the Bratva feels trivial compared to my past losses.

If it weren't for Kass, who has been my anchor during these turbulent times, I honestly can't imagine where I would find myself today.

Her support has made all the difference.

The day I walked into the nail salon was the day I was ready to kill myself.

I had it all planned out, but I just wanted to do something nice for myself before I ended my life.

Kass and Asia came through for me during what felt like one of the most challenging times in my life.

Their support was like a lifeline, helping me step back from the edge of a dark place I was in.

When I finally met their husbands, the experience was surprisingly welcoming; they embraced me as part of their circle, making me feel accepted and valued.

As the head bartender at Kastaways, I'm deeply invested in the art of mixology and the vibrant atmosphere of the bar, but I want to be absolutely clear about my stance regarding the underhanded dealings that are often associated with the Bratva.

I've made a deliberate choice to steer clear of that murky world.

When Kass approached me about it, I was straightforward—I expressed my desire to remain blissfully unaware of its inner workings unless my safety or job was directly jeopardized.

My daily focus is refreshingly uncomplicated: I craft cocktails that tantalize the taste buds, engage with patrons to create a welcoming ambiance, and diligently earn my paycheck.

That's the scope of my involvement—purely about the drinks and the people who enjoy them.

As a bartender, I weave my way through two distinct sections of the club, each exuding its own captivating ambiance. The majority of my shifts find me upstairs at the main bar, immersed in the lively chatter and infectious energy that fills the air.

The laughter and clinking of glasses create a vibrant tapestry of sounds as patrons revel in the night's festivities.

Occasionally, I have the chance to slip away from this bustling scene and venture down into the alluring underground sex club.

This hidden sanctuary pulses with a seductive rhythm, its dim lighting, and enigmatic atmosphere offering a stark contrast to the upper level.

Here, the air is thick with intrigue, and the excitement is palpable, inviting exploration and adventure in ways that are both daring and exhilarating.

Each visit to this clandestine space feels like stepping into another world, where boundaries are pushed and secrets unearthed.

Do I participate in social events and gatherings?

No, not really.

Do I want to?

Absolutely, yes.

When I reflect on my sexual experiences, I realize they have been relatively brief yet deeply significant.

Throughout my life, I have shared intimate moments with only three individuals, each experience leaving a unique imprint on my journey.

The memories of these encounters are vivid, marked by their own emotions and contexts, shaping my understanding of intimacy and connection in distinct ways.

My first partner, Chance Connor, holds a special place in my memories, one that is bittersweet and complex.

Our time together was filled with moments of joy and laughter, but it was ultimately marred by the heartbreak he inflicted.

When our relationship ended, it felt as if a part of me had shattered, along with my trust in him.

The pain of that breakup still leaves a lingering imprint on my heart, a reminder of what once was.

Even though the hurt he caused me was profound, I genuinely hope that life has smiled upon him since we parted ways.

I often find myself wishing the best for him despite the memories that still flood my mind—memories of our shared laughter and dreams, now tinged with sorrow.

I've worked hard to find a place of forgiveness in my heart for what transpired between us, yet the echoes of those experiences refuse to fade entirely.

I carry those vivid recollections with me, each one a testament to the lessons learned and the love once shared, even as I struggle to let go completely.

The other two partners I've had were more laid-back and less meaningful in the grand scheme of things.

Gabe, for instance, is someone I still encounter from time to time. He's become something of a familiar presence at Kastaways, the cozy local bar we both love to visit.

When the desire for physical connection strikes us—what I sometimes refer to as an "itch to be scratched"—we don't hesitate to reach out to each other.

Yet, it's been nearly two months since we last engaged in that familiar, intimate dance of ours, and I can't help but feel that lingering sense of longing.

Then there's Rod, who was briefly a part of my life but turned out to be an unfortunate mistake.

What was supposed to be a casual fling quickly spiraled into something much darker. Our time together ended on a particularly sour note that left a bitter taste in my mouth.

He hasn't reached out to me in ages, and I haven't seen him at Kastaways in quite some time, which I believe is for the best.

Rod was banned from the establishment following a shocking incident where he laced my drink during one of our outings. It was a violation of trust that shattered any hope for a future between us and left me questioning everything I thought I knew about him.

The experience was not only frightening but also deeply unsettling, making it clear that our connection was toxic from the very beginning.

The Bratva members take our safety very seriously, and they don't mess around when it comes to threats.

While he might be prohibited from stepping foot in this place, the consequences could just as easily lead him to a grave six feet deep.

Working at Kastaways comes with its own dangers, but the potential rewards and protection we receive far outweigh the risks involved.

I adore my job, but I yearn to be loved deep down.

I often daydream about my youth, when I was a carefree teenager hopelessly devoted to one person.

Those moments when love felt so pure and uncomplicated are something I long to experience again.

I desire someone who will embrace me for every facet of who I am, even the parts that feel fractured and vulnerable.

My heart has endured so much pain; it has been torn apart more times than I can count—by men who didn't appreciate me and by the profound loss of my parents.

Each heartbreak has left its mark, but I still hold onto hope.

Despite the challenges in my personal life, I've discovered a sense of joy in my career as a bartender.

It has become a sanctuary for me, a place where I find fulfillment and happiness.

Through my work, I've forged new friendships and unearthed aspects of myself that I never knew existed, growing more confident with each passing day.

Surrounding me are incredible women who serve as role models—strong, inspiring figures whose qualities I admire and aspire to emulate.

I understand that personal growth takes time, but I am determined to carve out my identity and blossom into the person I want to be.

I believe that, with patience and resilience, I will eventually come into my own.

If I could travel back in time, I would passionately strive to alter several pivotal moments in my life.

Firstly, my thoughts would undoubtedly center around the day I lost my parents. I would move heaven and earth to ensure they were safe and sound. I would make it my mission to create an impenetrable shield around them, to protect them from the tragic fate that awaited us that night. I envision bringing them joy, spoiling them with all the love and care they had given me throughout my childhood. We would create new memories together, moments filled with laughter, warmth, and cherished conversations that would last a lifetime. I would do everything in my power to keep our family whole and fill our home with their light and love again.

Secondly, my heart would urge me to fight fiercely for my first love.

I would seize every opportunity to reach out to make my feelings known without reservation. Instead of letting uncertainty hold me back, I would reply to his last text message without hesitation, pouring my heart into my words.

I would incessantly call him, determined to have a conversation that would unravel our misunderstandings.

I wouldn't allow him to escape without facing me; I would demand the honesty and connection we once shared.

The fear of taking risks would no longer hinder me; I would be ready to embrace vulnerability, even if it meant facing the possibility of rejection.

Ultimately, this retrospective reflection drives a profound realization: it's time to reclaim my narrative.

Even if it leads me down a path where I might never find enduring love or must continue bartending indefinitely, I would prioritize my needs and desires.

This newfound resolve would empower me to chase after the life I want, taking control of my destiny rather than being a mere spectator in my own story.

The last time I felt special was when Chance whispered to me, "Your name should be Tori, with an I because every time I see you, my heart screams mine."

From then on, whenever I'm asked, my name is T-O-R-I.

Chapter 2

Connor

Six years ago, I made a decision that would forever alter the course of my life.

In a moment of cold detachment, I chose to break up with my first love, Tori, through a simple text message.

Tori was everything to me—more essential than the very air I breathed.

From the moment we met in the bustling hallways of our small-town high school, I knew there was something special about her.

She had an incredible ability to illuminate the best parts of me as if she possessed a kind of magic that allowed her to see the potential I often overlooked in myself.

Her laughter was like sunlight breaking through the clouds, brightening even my darkest days, and her encouragement pushed me to strive for goals I never thought I could achieve.

Tori was not just my first love; she was my confidante, the person I turned to when I needed advice or solace.

We shared secrets under the stars during lazy summer nights, mapping out dreams of the future that felt within our reach. Our conversations flowed effortlessly, ranging from silly anecdotes about our teenage dramas to deep discussions about our hopes and fears.

Every moment spent with her was an adventure, whether we were embarking on spontaneous road trips to nearby towns or simply exploring the hidden gems of our familiar surroundings.

With Tori by my side, even the ordinary felt extraordinary, and life was an exhilarating journey filled with laughter and discovery.

We shared unforgettable moments that are etched in my mind:

Our breathless first kiss, a rush of innocent joy and curiosity;

Our tentative first date, where laughter mingled with nervous glances;

Our first sleepover, the thrill of the night wrapped in whispered secrets and stolen touches;

And that defining moment when we lost our virginity to each other, an experience marked by both fear and elation.

But then everything changed when I turned twenty-three.

My father presented me with a harsh ultimatum, one that felt like a noose tightening around my neck.

He offered me a choice: I could step into his world, take over the family business, and marry a woman of his choosing, or I could sever my ties with Tori and walk away with two million dollars, fully aware that I would never be able to contact either of them again.

To my father, Tori represented everything that was beneath our family—she was not just beneath our wealth but, in his eyes, beneath the image he worked so hard to maintain.

He valued status and money above all else.

In a moment of desperation, I chose the money and the promise of freedom from my father's control, even though I knew that this choice would shatter Tori's heart into a million pieces.

I broke up with her through a cold and impersonal text, a decision I would later come to regret, knowing the pain it would cause to someone who had meant so much to me.

"We are not meant to be. I am moving. I hope to meet you again later in life. C"

As I pressed send, my phone screen cracked into a web of shattered glass, mirroring the chaos in my mind.

My heart raced, heavy with guilt and fear. I couldn't bear to face her, knowing she would use her soft voice to coax me into staying.

Deep down, I feared for her safety; my dad had a way of turning love into cruelty.

I envisioned him coming after her, unleashing a torment that would leave scars far more profound than any physical wound.

It was a nightmare I couldn't allow to happen.

For years, my father had worn his disappointment like a shroud, his eyes reflecting the shame he felt towards me.

"You'll never live up to my expectations," he'd often say, words that cut sharper than any knife.

The warmth and affection that once filled our home vanished the day my mother passed away.

That tragic moment marked a profound turning point in his demeanor; it was as if a switch had been flipped inside him.

The warmth and affection of the loving father I once knew was abruptly replaced by the cold, cutthroat persona of a tyrannical warden.

He began enforcing his rules with an unyielding iron fist, leaving no room for negotiation or dissent.

His rigid expectations dictated every aspect of our lives, and in that stifling, oppressive atmosphere, I could feel my spirit slowly being crushed.

The weight of his demands pressed down on me, making it hard to breathe, and I found myself longing for the days when love and understanding had reigned in our home.

One fateful day, I found myself holding onto the hope that she might one day forgive me.
If our paths were to intertwine again by some twist of fate, I would spare no effort to make amends and rectify the hurt I caused her.

She truly deserves the world, and I long to offer her all that I can.

I constantly grapple with the weight of my choice, tormented by the knowledge that I failed to be there like I promised I would be.

In the years that followed, I have yet to encounter a love that even remotely resembles what we once shared. The depth of that connection remains unmatched in my heart, a bittersweet reminder of what we had and what was lost.

I intentionally avoid conventional relationships, opting instead for more pragmatic arrangements. In these encounters, love, emotions, and romantic gestures are absent; it's simply about two consenting adults meeting each other's needs in a practical and straightforward manner.

My experiences with women have frequently been brief and transient, leaving little room for deeper emotional connections to develop. Each woman I've engaged with has often served a specific purpose—whether to satisfy a fleeting longing or to provide a momentary escape from the routine and monotony of my everyday life. As I reflect on these past interactions, a wave of nostalgia envelops me, leading me to wonder if I will ever encounter someone who can rival the impact of Tori. She occupies a unique space in my memories, an unwavering benchmark against which I find myself measuring the women who come and go in my life.

Although each woman possesses her own unique qualities, none have resonated with me on the same profound level that Tori once did. The connections I've made—though they may have been exciting or pleasurable at the moment—inevitably serve as a stark reminder of the void she left behind. This lingering absence deepens my curiosity about the possibility of finding a love that feels truly genuine and profound, one that could potentially fill the space that Tori once occupied in my heart. It's a lingering question that hovers in my mind, fueling the search for something more meaningful amidst the ephemeral moments of my current arrangements.

My thoughts drift to her, and I can't help but wonder where she might be now.

Did she finally set off on the thrilling adventures she always talked about, traversing the globe to explore distant lands and immerse herself in vibrant cultures, just as she longed to do?

Has she discovered a kindred spirit, someone who holds her heart and exchanged vows in a beautiful ceremony, stepping into the next chapter of her life enveloped in love, laughter, and the warmth of shared dreams?

Did she transform her aspiration of owning a stunning home into a tangible reality, crafting a sanctuary filled with warmth and character, adorned exactly to her liking, reflecting her personality in every room?

What fuels her passion these days? Is she chasing a career that ignites her spirit and drives her ambitions, or perhaps delving into hobbies that bring her profound joy and a sense of fulfillment, allowing her creativity to flourish?

Most importantly, is she surrounded by a circle of love, feeling cherished and valued by friends, embraced by the affection of those who uplift her?

I know I should focus on the present and refrain from dwelling on the past, yet it's incredibly difficult to forget the vibrant memories that shaped my upbringing.

Today, I oversee a diverse portfolio of businesses, navigating both legal enterprises and more unconventional ventures.

Having carved out my own unique journey, I have stepped into the light of my own identity, no longer confined to the imposing shadow of my father's esteemed legacy.

At the helm of CC Incorporated, I lead a dynamic corporation that encompasses a wide array of services, including publishing, financial advisement, and talent management.

Our mission is to empower creativity and drive success across various industries.

One of the most profitable companies that I help take care of is Balentine Industries.

I know all about their world; about two years ago, I was asked to join their ranks.

I help maintain their legal front with Valentine Industries, but also, when need be, I'm hired muscle.

Over the past three years, I have dedicated myself to a transformative journey that has led me to bulk up significantly.

Reflecting on my high school days, I remember being the scrawny, nerdy kid who often went unnoticed in the crowd.

Back then, I struggled with self-confidence and felt as if I didn't fit in with my peers.

However, through a combination of hard work, determination, and a stroke of good fortune, I have completely reinvented not just my physical appearance but also my entire life perspective.

Today, I stand tall as one of the world's top 100 self-made billionaires, which is a testament to my entrepreneurial spirit and unwavering drive for success.

This achievement is not just about financial wealth; it represents countless hours of dedication, learning from failures, and seizing opportunities as they came my way.

The journey has been incredible, filled with challenges that tested my resilience and milestones that celebrated my growth.

As I look toward the future, I feel a profound sense of excitement and motivation. I am eager to explore new ventures, inspire others who may feel overlooked, and continue on this path of self-improvement and entrepreneurial exploration.

The road ahead is bright, and I am ready to embrace whatever comes my way.

Aside from any potential connection with someone other than Torianne Sullivan, there is truly no one who can fill the profound void I feel in my heart for her.

The depth of our relationship is unmatched, and the bond we share is irreplaceable.

No matter who might enter my life, they could never fill the special place she holds within me.

Being a member of the Bratva certainly has its advantages.

Take tonight, for instance—I'm on the guest list for an exclusive VIP masquerade ball at Kastaways, a luxurious venue known for its opulence and intrigue.

The atmosphere will be electric, filled with the sound of laughter and soft music, while guests in elegant masks and exquisite attire mingle under the glow of elaborate chandeliers.

It's the perfect opportunity to rub shoulders with influential figures and perhaps strike a deal or two, all while keeping our identities shrouded in mystery.

In the three years I've been on Dorian's team, I have never set foot in Kastaways.

But he said there's something I need to see.

I know Kastaways is an elite club, a sex club for high rollers and big shots.

I told Dorian I did not want to go, but he said there's something I need to see, so I will go even for just a little bit, but I don't think I will participate in the elite activities unless someone catches my eye.

It's finally time to pull out my favorite suit, a perfectly tailored ensemble that fits me like a glove, complete with sleek lines and a striking color that always turns heads.

Paired with it is my custom mask, intricately designed to reflect my personality and style, featuring unique patterns and embellishments that make it truly one-of-a-kind.

Maybe I will be able to relax and unwind; let's take a chance.

Chapter 3

You have got to be kidding me!

Dorian and Hailey have decided that I can't work tonight, and it's such a shame because the VIP masquerade ball at Kastaways is happening.

I could really use the tips from such a busy night. Instead, Dorian insisted that if I show up to the masquerade, he'll compensate me by the hour, which, while tempting, isn't exactly what I had in mind.

I'll admit, the thought of mingling with a crowd makes me feel an unsettling knot in my stomach, but I can't ignore the fact that I have the perfect outfit ready for the occasion.

My elegant gown, a deep shade of purple that seems to shimmer with every movement, flows effortlessly to the floor, creating an ethereal silhouette.

The fabric is soft and luxurious against my skin, making me feel both empowered and beautiful.

To complement the gown, I wear a stunning mask that intricately matches the rich hue of my dress.

It is decorated with delicate silver filigree that sparkles subtly in the light.

The mask adds an air of mystery and intrigue, allowing me to blend into the enchanting atmosphere of the evening while still standing out.

Wearing purple has always made me feel whole and alive, and this particular dress feels as if it were made just for me, hugging my curves perfectly and allowing me to radiate confidence.

The purple sparkly dress hugs my torso, pushing my triple D breasts to the top of the corset for all to see.

However, the bottom of the dress flares out into a sparkly sea of tulle.

The thought of entering the venue, draped in elegance and mystery, is enticing.

What if I can find joy amid the chaos?

Even though I find myself grappling with my discomfort at the thought of being surrounded by unfamiliar faces, I can't help but feel the pulse of excitement in the air. Part of me is torn—should I let anxiety dictate my evening, or should I embrace the adventure and the enchanting night ahead?

The ambiance at Kastaways is vibrant and lively tonight, with the first-floor bustling with activity.

Guests are packed closely together, creating a warm and social atmosphere filled with the sound of laughter and conversation. Couples lean close to share intimate whispers while singles navigate through the crowd, eagerly engaging in friendly banter.

The enticing aroma of gourmet dishes wafts through the air, drawing everyone in with promises of culinary delights.

Although I feel at ease in this lively setting, a powerful sense of curiosity beckons me toward the second floor.

The allure of what awaits above tugs at me, compelling me to leave the familiarity of the crowd behind.

Each time I work on the second floor, I feel completely flushed and embarrassed, as if I were experiencing the dark and luring atmosphere for the first time.

The atmosphere up there is charged with unmistakable energy; it's apparent that everyone who steps onto that level possesses a sense of awareness and a strong grasp of their desires and needs.

It's as if the space itself buzzes with unspoken understanding, leaving me somewhat overwhelmed and very much aware of the confident dynamics around me.

I embrace the fullness of my curvaceous body, feeling satisfied in my skin.

However, I can't help but notice that the crowd on the second floor carries an air of effortless confidence that I still strive to achieve.

The mask feels like a blessing tonight. It allows me to blend into the crowd without fear of being recognized, and it gives me a strange sense of security as if I can slip into another version of myself, even if just for a little while.

As I make my way to the bar, the atmosphere hums with laughter and music, inviting me to let loose. I settle onto one of the plush barstools, grateful for the anonymity that comes with the dim lighting and buzz of conversation.

This moment of solitude is a welcome reprieve, and the relief washes over me as I glance around, reassured that no one seems to be paying me any mind.

Just then, Shannon, the lively bartender with a warm smile and a keen eye for detail, spots me.

She glides over, her voice playful as she places a drink in front of me. "Here you go, Violet. It's not from me, though. It's from the gentleman at the far end of the bar. I'd say the two of you are destined to share more than just a drink tonight."

Intrigued, I turn my gaze to the other end of the bar. As my eyes land on him, my heart skips a beat. There's something magnetic about his presence, almost otherworldly. Those piercing eyes hold a depth that captivates me, making the rest of the world fade into the background. The anticipation of what could unfold sends a rush of exhilaration through me.

It's been years since I've felt this kind of spark.

There's something magnetic about him.

He's wearing a striking violet suit that fits like a glove, complemented by a shimmering silvery shirt beneath.

With the top two buttons undone, I catch a glimpse of his curly chest hair peeking out, adding to his alluring presence.
Be
Reaching into my pocket, I pulled out the only cash I had brought with me, feeling a rush of excitement.

"Shannon," I called, my voice steady, "please make him my signature drink. And tell him to bring his drink down here if he's interested in joining me."

Shannon teases with a playful smirk dancing on her lips, "Violet, you've got it! You need to let loose tonight—seriously, I want to see you dragging yourself in tomorrow."

I let out a light laugh, raising an eyebrow with mock indignation, "Yes, momma! I promise I'll be on my best behavior... or maybe my worst!"

As I take a moment to reflect, the anticipation for the evening bubbles up inside me. Tonight is meant to be unforgettable, a whirlwind of music, laughter, and perhaps a touch of mischief.

In this vibrant scene, everyone knows me as Violet, my cherished nickname that I adopt for all club events.

It's a name that seems to summon good fortune; let's hope it carries a sprinkle of magic that turns any ordinary night into an extraordinary adventure.

Chapter 4

Connor

That curvy body turns heads, drawing gazes that sweep left and right like moths to a flame.

She is a purple angel, radiating an aura that seems to cast a permanent glow around her as if she's been plucked from some enchanting realm where she reigns supreme.

Shannon, the cute and quirky bartender, glides over to me with a playful smile.

"Violet asked me to bring you this drink," she says, her eyes twinkling.

"She mentioned it comes with an invitation to join her. But don't worry—she won't hold it against you if you decide to pass. The drink she picked for you is called Heart of Chance. It's our head bartender's specialty, crafted with blueberry rum, crushed blackberries, a sprinkle of shimmering purple edible glitter, and a splash of coconut rum. Enjoy!"

I examine the vibrant concoction, intrigued by its allure.

What kind of woman would dream up something so unique, and why name it Heart of Chance?

With a faint smile, I raise my drink to toast the air before walking toward the princess.

She radiates an undeniable charm, a siren whose presence makes every man feel fortunate to have her by his side.

Her body, a captivating symphony of curves and grace, draws me in with an irresistible pull.

I find myself unable to tear my gaze away, nor can I summon the will to step back.

She seems to possess the power to entwine my very soul, holding me in her thrall as if she could capture me completely and never release her grip.

I slyly lean on the bar next to her, "I appreciate the drink. What brings you here tonight? The bartender said your name is Violet, is that right?"

She slyly smirks, "That is my name here. The color purple brings me joy."

Odd, that sounds familiar.

"I get it. You want to remain anonymous. You can call me CC, just the letters. You still haven't answered my question: What brings you here tonight?"

The smirk lingers playfully on her lips.

"Here I am, being compelled to partake in this company-mandated revelry. My boss insisted I take a break and unwind, claiming I work far too hard. So, against my will, I've been dragged into this little soiree. They know all too well that Mardi Gras holds no appeal for me."

Interesting, she's not from here.

"Oh, I see now—you're not originally from good old Mississippi. Mardi Gras really embodies the spirit of the South, doesn't it? With vibrant beads, lively celebrations, cold beers in hand, and extravagant balls, it's an experience unlike any other. You'd better be ready for the playful chaos where people throw all those things at you! But trust me, I totally understand; Mardi Gras was quite the cultural adjustment for me, too, when I first arrived here. So, do you work around here? If you don't mind me asking, what's your role? You must have developed a close rapport with Dorian; he's quite the character! How's he treating you? I hope it's been a good experience!"

Her eyes glimmer, "He's a real gentleman; Hailey would have his balls if he wasn't. I'm the head bartender. Kass hired me years ago. I helped open the place. That drink you're drinking is a concoction of mine; it's called Heart of Chance. It's a drink that gives me confidence when I need it."

Wow, she's been with Kastaways since its inception, and she is a true veteran of the organization.

It's a curious coincidence that we both joined the Bratva around the same time, weaving our paths into this clandestine world together.

"So, you're familiar with the Pakhan?" I inquired, intrigued by the connections she might have.

She let out a light, melodic laugh, her eyes sparkling with mischief.

"Oh, I certainly know the Pakhan. If you ever dared to call him that to his face, I would love to witness it! He's far too laid-back for such a title—he prefers simply being called 'boss.'"

I couldn't help but think about her ties with Massimo and Kassani.

She casually referred to Kassani as "Kass," which made me wonder just how deep their friendship runs.

What additional responsibilities and roles does she undertake within the complex and shadowy operations of the Bratva?

I lean in closer, my breath warm against her ear, and growl playfully, "What delightful mischief can we weave together?"

With wide eyes and an excited smile, she gasps, "Let's host an unforgettable ball of our own! I can get the key to the mysterious Violet Room—it's hidden behind that ancient bookshelf in the library. Just imagine it: a night filled with elegant masks and twinkling chandeliers. Are you ready to join me for some masked fun and create a night full of secrets and enchantment?"

Oh, Violet, I have my doubts about whether you could manage even a single night of this adventure.

"By all means, take the lead, Lady Violet."

Chapter 5

Tori

6 Years Ago....

(One week before my parents died...)

It was our cherished weekly date night, a tradition that always filled my heart with joy.

We had just returned from a delightful dinner at our favorite diner, an enchanting spot that felt like a cozy oasis amid the bustling streets of New York City.

Diners are becoming increasingly rare in this urban landscape, making those moments spent at our beloved eatery even more special.

Now, we found ourselves nestled in the back of Connor's truck, the cool night air wrapping around us like a gentle embrace as we lay beneath a sky blanketed in shimmering stars.

The distant glow of city lights flickered around the edges of Central Park, contrasting beautifully with the vast darkness above.

"The dark can never dim our love, Tore," he said, his voice tender and sincere.

He pulled me closer as if to shield me from the world.

How sweet is my man?!

"I know, Chance. I can see our love enduring through lifetimes," I replied, my heart swelling with an affection that felt as infinite as the sky above us.

In that magical moment, I realized that no force could ever reclaim my heart from Chance; it was forever entwined with his, bound by an unbreakable connection that only deepened with each passing starry night.

"When are you going to marry me?" he asked, his voice steady yet filled with a hint of vulnerability.

What?!

The question hung in the air like a delicate whisper, sending my heart racing.

"Connor, you really want to spend forever with me?"

I gazed into his eyes, searching for confirmation of this beautiful madness.

A rush of warmth flooded through me, making it hard to breathe.

My heart couldn't handle all this sweetness.

I let out a soft sigh, the weight of his words settling around me like a warm embrace. "If you're asking, then my answer will always be yes."

"Why don't we take the plunge and get married next week, right on our cherished date night?"

He trails gentle, tender kisses along the curve of my neck, sending shivers down my spine.

My mind becomes a whirlwind of thoughts, all muddled and chaotic, as his warm lips linger against my skin, making it impossible to think clearly.

But my love is anything but jumbled.

"Let's embark on this journey together! Just you and me, hand in hand, embracing the adventure that lies ahead! You and I, forever and always, bound by a promise that knows no end!"

5 Days Later…

My life is truly a dream come true, and it feels even more wonderful than I could have ever imagined!

In just two days, I will be marrying Connor, the love of my life!

We've decided to kick off our journey together with a special date night, followed by our visit to the courthouse to exchange our vows!

My parents adore Connor and are eagerly looking forward to welcoming him into our family as their son-in-law!

My phone buzzes softly, a gentle vibration that interrupts the quiet moment.

Connor's name suddenly lights up the screen in bold letters, and an unexpected rush of excitement courses through me.

Why do I suddenly feel like a giddy schoolgirl, heart racing and cheeks warming at the thought of him?

My heart shatters into a million fragile pieces as I read his text, each word cutting deeper than the last…

"We are not meant to be. I am moving. I hope to meet you again later in life. C"

The finality of his message hangs in the air, heavy with unspoken emotions and a bittersweet promise of what could have been.

I quickly tapped out a response, my heart racing as I felt a wave of disbelief wash over me.

"You're joking?! How did we get here? Call me!" I hit send, hoping for an immediate reply.

I stared at my phone, anxiety knotting my stomach. The screen seemed to taunt me with its stark, cold message: "NOT DELIVERED."

It felt like an unwelcome punchline to a cruel joke, intensifying the uncertainty that was swirling around me.

Ok, fuck you, Connor Chance!

I will never again allow myself to be swept away by the intoxicating spell of love, like a moth drawn to a flame.

Connor

"We are not meant to be. I am moving. I hope to meet you again later in life. C"

As soon as I hit send, a wave of regret washed over me.

I blocked her number, unable to face the reality of what I had just done. In a fit of anger and despair, I threw my phone into the tumultuous ocean, watching it sink beneath the waves, taking with it the one connection that brought me happiness.

Now, I feel an overwhelming void, as if a part of me has been lost forever.

Tori was my light, my joy, and I let her slip away without a fight.

My dad will pay for all the hurt and mistakes he's caused; I swear justice will come.

I can't shake the feeling that if I'd only had the courage to fight for Tori, things might have turned out differently.

If I ever get another chance, I promise I won't let it slip through my fingers again.

Chapter 6

Tori

(Present day)

"There's a library?" CC inquires; his curiosity evident.

I chuckle softly, a lightness dancing in my voice.

"We refer to it as a library, but it's really just a solitary bookshelf strategically placed to disguise the Violet Room. By the way, I should probably ask if you have any kinks or limits."

He shrugs casually, an enigmatic smile playing on his lips.

"I wouldn't know how to answer that. Can we discover them together?"

His words send a flutter of warmth through me. I quickly shake off the feeling.

"Whatever you desire, CC, but only for tonight! I'm not looking for anything more."

It's vital that he understands this is just playful escapism—emotions are no longer a part of my equation.

I steadfastly refuse to allow myself to fall in love again.

The complexities and heartaches that accompany love simply aren't worth the endless struggle it brings! Instead, I choose to embrace the thrill of life, where joy and fun take center stage.

Love needs to find someone else to bother.

I have the key to the library; I drag CC to the library.

As we open the bookshelf door, his eyes go wide.

Inside are just a few contraptions, and his shocked expression conveys that he was not prepared for me.

He was not prepared for someone like me to have kinks.

I am always judged here due to my size.

"This is what you're into?" CC asks.

I give him the stink eye, "Meaning what?"

He gulps, "Meaning, do you understand what this world entails, little girl? It is not a game. Men, women, and all couples have signed many contracts to enter kinky partnerships. Is that what you are looking for?"
So he's not judging me?

He just asked me what I am looking for.

Odd.

"I am looking for fun, not a relationship. I will not allow my heart to be shattered again. I want a memorable night, and that's all I am asking for. You don't have to use any contraptions in this Room. You can ravage me up against this wall. Are you in or out? If you are out, there's the door?"

Connor

She is sassy. She makes me want to spank her and show her who's boss.

I smirk, "Little girl, I am not someone to play with. But I respect your openness and your honesty. Little girl, I haven't had a relationship in a long time. I am here just like you are; it is mandatory fun. So I am in if you are. But remember little girl, I am in the Bratva. So play at your own risk."

"Fine by me, CC. But after tonight, you will never call me a little girl again! I am all woman, and I will prove it. Watch out. You might get burned!"

Fire.

Whit.

Pure SASS.

"Which, as you said, contraption do you want to try? Be warned, I have a heavy hand."

She blushes for the first time all night. There is the little girl who has been hiding all night.

"No contraptions tonight. Just us, just fun. We have this Room for an hour and a half. The only contraption you can use is your joystick."

She knows what she wants, but she is giving me newbie vibes.

She may not have had much or any kink experience, but that just excites me more.

I sigh and stalk towards her.

"You."

STEP

"Want."

"Fun."

STEP

"With?"

STEP

"Me."

Her back hits the violet wall.

Her eyes glitter with anticipation.

There is no fear or panic there, just lust and need.

I lean against the wall and place my hand above her head.

"Are you ready for me? Last chance to Run, little girl."

Before she responds, I hear a zipper.

Her dress hits the floor.

"Fun is my middle name. But can you handle a fluffy woman? There's no little girl here. I am a whole dessert to wash down your drink."

My breath hitches.

Woman is an understatement, Goddess is more like it.

Curves for days.

Thighs that I would let smother me any day!

Bare breasts that are perfectly perky but will spill out of my hands.

She has to be a D or more; I want my face to be lost in them!

I feel my emotions rising…

Why do I feel anything right now?

Be her dangerous escape.

Give her the fun she thinks she craves.

I unbutton my shirt, then slip off my belt.

"Goddess, you can use my joystick however you see fit."
I snap my belt like a whip.

She didn't flinch or break eye contact.

She points to the vintage loveseat.

She slips out of her shoes.

"Lay down; I'm going enjoy this ride. This Goddess is either going to send you to heaven or hell. Make your choice, CC!"

Goddess, I will follow you anywhere.

"Earth is hell; take me to your heaven."

Violet pushes me toward the loveseat.

"As enticing as those skin-tight pants are, they would look better on the floor."

 Well damn!

You don't have to tell me twice!

Boss me!

Direct me!

Kiss me!

Just give me tonight!

Chapter 7

Cc embodies attractiveness in every sense, radiating a captivating charisma that draws people in effortlessly.

From their striking features and confident demeanor to their magnetic personality, CC captures the attention and admiration of those around them.

Women were trying to get his attention left and right when we were in the club, but somehow, his eyes were locked on me.

I have to stop myself from drooling.

His pants hit the floor, and I had to snap my mouth shut.

Hot damn!

This man is ripped!

Round bulging pecks, a six-pack of abs I just want to lick!

His Bratva tattoo sprawls boldly across his left pectoral, an intricate emblem of his allegiance, yet beneath it lies a jagged scar—a silent testament to the pain endured.

I once knew someone who bore a similar mark in that very spot, a haunting reminder of a heartbroken past I'd rather forget.

I forcefully clear those memories from my mind; he doesn't deserve even a fleeting thought. My lust for CC is growing.

I feel the wetness running down my thighs.

I slip my purple lacy thong off.

"Are you clean, CC?"

His chuckle flows down my spine, "Violet, I'm a member of the Bratva. Dorian makes us get tested just to walk through the door. Are you clean?"

I smile, "I work here, and I'm held to the same standard. Not that it matters, but I haven't been with anyone recently because I am married to my job. Also, I have a birth control implant in my arm, so there is no need to hold back the joy from your stick."

"Then let's get this ball rolling!"

He pulls me onto the loveseat with him.

"Use me for your pleasure, Violet. I am at your mercy, Goddess."

That whispered phrase sent my lust into overdrive!

I start kissing down his neck, taking my time and dragging out each kiss.

I go from his neck to his shoulder.

Then, from his shoulder to his pectorals.

A flood of memories of Connor rushes back to me, each one vivid and sharp.

The way he used to laugh, throw his head back, and reveal that charming dimple plays in my mind like a favorite song.

Yet, along with the warmth of those recollections comes a wave of frustration.

The moments we shared, filled with both joy and heartache, haunt me now, taunting me with what was lost.

It's infuriating to feel so tethered to the past, even as I crave a future unclouded by the shadows of his memory.

I swiftly redirect my attention to the striking man lying before me; his features captivating in the soft glow of the light.

His deep-set eyes hold a mysterious allure while a gentle smile plays on his lips, enhancing the charm he effortlessly exudes.

I give into my intrusive thought and lick his delicious abs!

I would love to lick some chocolate off of them!

My lips slide down to his deep V, and he automatically gasps.

Now we are getting somewhere!

I love it when men get noisy during sex, and it's a big turn-on for me.

It gives me the encouragement I need to keep going.

It's time to see if CC likes oral.

I snake my tongue down his V and around his shaft.

He tastes so sweet and smooth.

His body cries out for my tongue; he can't be still.

His crotch is arching into my mouth.

He is loud, just like I crave.

"Fuck! Goddess, I could come like this! Your mouth is pure heaven!"

I need more from him!

His praise is making me squirm.

His moans fill the room and my ears.

I can taste how close he is.

I tease his shaft with the softness of my pelvis.

I rub my wetness along his shaft.

"Stop fucking teasing me, Goddess!"

He snatches my hips and impales me with his shaft.

There is no time for me to prepare myself.

"FUCK! You better fill me up! FUCK, CC!"

I had no control over the words that slipped out.

He has taken control of our scene and my body.

His thrusts are getting harder and faster.

"Yes! Yes! I will feel you to the brim!"

I feel my orgasm building.

"FUCK! Come, CC! FUCK!"

I feel the earthquake hit me!

He doesn't let up.

He makes sure we both make it to the shattering point.

I collapse on top of him, completely breathless, feeling the weight of the moment as my heart races.

I've never experienced anything like that before— each sensation was electrifying, igniting a fire within me that I didn't know existed.

"Can we do this again?" I whisper, my voice trembling with a mix of exhilaration and uncertainty.

I know he didn't hear me; I was quieter than a mouse.

It's clear to me now: he may have just ruined me for any other man, leaving me craving his touch, his voice, and the way he understands every part of me.

Chapter 8

Connor

As she rests upon me, I steal a glance at my watch.

Our intimate exchange has lingered for thirty minutes, a duration that hovers somewhere between commendable and disappointing.

Though I sense a hint of self-consciousness in her demeanor, perhaps due to her size, it doesn't alter my perception in the slightest.

To me, her body is not a measure of beauty; it is simply a part of the connection we share.

She shattered me with just her tongue; I had to take control just to get her to give in.

It's like someone broke her.

I glance at my watch again; our hour and a half is drawing to a close.

I kiss her forehead.

"Goddess, we have fifteen minutes left before they come looking for the key to the library."

She looked at me with those doe eyes, and only then did I realize that we had kept our masks on during our scene.

Why do her doe eyes seem familiar?

She stretches, "No worries. We have time. I'll shoot Shannon a quick text."

She slowly untangles her luscious body from mine and stands up.

"So, Goddess, did that scene take you to heaven or hell?"

She shrugs, "I was definitely close to the gates, but I won't say which one."

She is just flirting with me.

Her body told me everything I needed to know when she came.

Keep it to yourself, Goddess.

I know exactly what your body told me.

"What was it that you were screaming and moaning? Oh, that's right, my name."

She giggles, "I get it CC. You're an old man who's been around the block. I have got to get going. This was the fun that I needed!"

"It was a pleasure, Goddess. Let me know if you want to get together for fun again; Dorian knows exactly how to find me."

She huffs," Do not get your hopes up, CC. This was everything that I needed and more! But I told you fun is all I need."

Why do I feel like she just dismissed me?

She reaches for her thong and then stalks to her dress.

I see some little writing on her shoulder blade.

There's a heart, and then the words make my chest tighten.

"Every time I see you, my heart screams mine."

I was there when she got that tattoo.

This could be my second chance...

Chapter 9

Four and a half years ago...

Date night is the night I look forward to every week.

Tonight, Tore said she wants to take a big step.

She wants to get a tattoo.

I asked her if she wanted us to get matching ones, and her response made me chuckle.

"Chance, only if that's what your heart tells you to do!"

That gave me the idea for our tattoos.

We each drew each other a heart; then, we picked a phrase that we loved.

Tore's said, "Every time I see you, my heart screams mine."

She placed the heart in front of the phrase.

My phrase reads, "I do what my heart tells me."

I put the heart she drew at the end, and she even wrote a "TC" in it.

When we show up at the tattoo parlor, they are ready for us as soon as we walk in.

I whisper," Are you sure this is what you want?"

Her doe eyes show me her heart.

"This is a big commitment, Chance. But this is the first step; the next commitment we will make is us walking down the aisle."

I kiss her forehead, " Anything for you, my heart!"

She makes me be the best man I can be.

She reminds me every chance she gets that I am not my father, and I don't have to be.

She squeezes my hand as she gets her tattoo right below her left shoulder blade.

"I love you, Chance."

I smile, "My love for you will surpass heaven and hell."

When her tattoo is done, she looks in the mirror and says, " It makes me feel like your arms are always around me."

All my emotions surge within me, a tidal wave of feelings crashing over my heart.

At that moment, I realized there was only one way to express the turmoil inside me.

I lean in closer, closing the distance between us, and press my lips against hers with an urgency that surprises even me.

My heart races as I deepen the kiss, swirling my tongue around hers, seeking connection and understanding in the warmth of our closeness.

The world around us fades, leaving just the two of us enveloped in a shared silence filled with unspoken words.

The warmth of love envelops me as her arms encircle my body, allowing our shared emotions to intertwine like an intricate dance.

I never imagined a heart as unblemished and radiant as hers would be devoted to me.

She clasped my hand firmly, offering unwavering support as the tattoo needle buzzed to life, etching my desires into my skin.

Though she initially doubted my resolve to inscribe the initials within a heart, I surprised her and myself by following through.

It was my heart, my Tore, that guided me toward this declaration—a testament to our bond.

Chapter 10

Connor

(Present Day)

The nickname slips out of my mouth before I can snap my mouth shut.

"Tore?"

She visibly stiffens, "What? Repeat that?"

She doesn't turn around.

I understand she's doing her best to shield her heart from further pain and disappointment.

Yet, she deserves to realize that my intentions are genuine and that it's truly me who cares deeply for her.

I want her to see that I'm here, ready to support and cherish her without any hidden motives.

This is my opportunity for redemption, my second chance at love and happiness.

I am determined to fight for her with everything I have this time.

I won't make the same mistakes as before; I will not let her slip away from me again.

I will show her my commitment through my actions, prove that I am worthy of her trust, and create the future we both deserve.

I take off my mask, "Tore, it's me."

Before she turns around, she starts to say, "Who is me? Only one person in the world has ever called me Tore. That person, whose voice still echoes in my mind, was responsible for shattering my sense of self—breaking me down into fragments I struggled to piece back together. Their betrayal cut deeper than any physical wound, making me question my worth and my will to live. In the darkest moments that followed, I found myself standing at the precipice of despair, overwhelmed by a suffocating weight that nearly pushed me to end it all. The scars of that experience remain etched in my heart, a constant reminder of the pain inflicted by someone I once trusted completely. Should I turn around and let my heart shatter all over again?"

She keeps her back turned, the tension in the air palpable.

I can sense that she is slowly shutting herself off from me, retreating into a shell that I may never penetrate.

The weight of her silence hangs heavy between us, a reminder of the darkness she has faced.

Did she really try to end her life?

The thought sends a chill through me, filling me with a mix of concern and helplessness.

She swiftly zips up her dress, the sound of the fabric sliding against itself sharp and final, and then carelessly tosses her mask onto the floor, its fall mirroring the weight of the moment.

Although she stands just in front of me, her gaze remains stubbornly averted.

I can see the pain etched in her posture, a silent testament to the hurt I never fully understood.

The depth of her distress hits me like a cold wave, leaving me grappling with the realization of just how far I've gone to cause this rift between us.

"This has to be a cruel trick being played on me! Tell me, CC, what is your name?"

I take a deep breath and sigh, "Connor Chance, or the woman I never stopped loving, would just call me Chance."

She swiftly snaps around to look at me.

As soon as her gaze locks onto mine, the facade of strength she had so carefully constructed collapses like a house of cards.

She crumples to the floor, her body wracked with sobs and pleads, "Please tell me you're a ghost, a fleeting specter who will vanish into the shadows. Tell me this is nothing more than a horrifying dream, that I didn't shatter my own heart yet again by committing the one act I swore I would never repeat. Why are you here? Don't you have Daddy's sprawling empire to manage?"

Of course, that's what she would remember.

"No, Tore. I chose to relinquish control of Daddy's Empire to forge my own path to become my own person. He presented me with a stark choice: take the reins of the empire or be disowned, left with just enough funds to launch my own venture. That day, my father issued a heart-wrenching ultimatum—if I didn't sever ties with you, he vowed to turn both your life and your parents' lives into a nightmare. So, with a heavy heart, I walked away, believing it would create a brighter future for you. I hoped you would find happiness with someone who truly deserves you. I am deeply sorry for the pain I've caused; that was never my intention. You have been, and always will be, the center of my thoughts."

The soft, heart-wrenching sobs escape her lips, each one resonating like a fragile shard of glass, piercing through the stillness and cracking my heart wide open.

"Three days!"

She screamed at me; Tore doesn't do that.

"THREE DAYS AFTER YOU WRIPPED MY HEART OUT MY PARENTS WERE KILLED! SO NO, I WILL NOT FORGIVE YOU! NO, YOU DON'T GET TO WALK BACK INTO MY LIFE! IF I KNEW IT, WAS YOU THIS WOULD HAVE NOT HAPPENED!"

She reaches under the desk and pushes the panic button.

Do I scare her that much?

"Tore, please give me a chance!"

"YOU DO NOT GET TO CALL ME THAT! SHE DIED THE DAY YOU LEFT ME!"

As I step towards her, Dorian comes in the room, "Don't step any closer, CC. Give her space. Go home I got her from here."

I barely hear Tore's whisper, "Call Kass, I am heading for the blackness."

Oh shit, I am screwed!

Kass will kill me if Tore tells her to fuck my life!

Chapter 11

Kass

My phone has been ringing off the hook a lot lately, so when it rings for the sixth time today, I don't even look at the name before answering.

"This better be good! I was just about to head to the gym!"

Dorian sighs, "I am sorry, my Queen! It is urgent."

"No worries, Dorian. What's going on? Is Hailey okay?"

"It's not Hailey, it's Tori. She asked me to call you and say that the black is back."

What?!

My heart starts beating fast; that's our code phrase!

We created that code phrase with all the Bratva girls so they can let us know if they are struggling.

"Damn it! Alright, take her to my apartment and make sure Hailey stays with her the entire time. I'm rearranging my schedule right now, and I'll be on my way in a few minutes. Make sure you don't let her out of your sight or Hailey's sight—she's really not in a good state of mind. Also, can you place an order for cherry chocolate ice cream and some sushi? Have that delivered to the apartment before I arrive. We need to make her as comfortable as possible. I'll meet you at the airport in two hours."

"Yes, my Queen. Are you sure the boss can handle being on his own?"

I chuckle softly, "He's made it through tough times before; he can manage just fine this time too."

"Yes, my Queen."

"Dorian quit being so formal! I am not the boss, but I appreciate the respect."

"No can do! Boss would have my balls, and so would Hailey. I need those!"

I can't hold back the rumbling laugh, "Okay, you got me there! I will see you soon."

As I hang up, I immediately text Tori, *"I am on my way! We will get through this together! Nothing is worth losing you! I love you!"*

I understand that she may not reply, but it's essential for her to recognize that she is not alone—I am here to support her unwaveringly. I refuse to let her descend into the shadows she once inhabited.

Tori has endured immense pain throughout her life; now, she deserves to embrace the tranquility she has long sought.

What could have set this off?

I am determined to uncover the truth—no one is allowed to hurt one of my girls and escape accountability.

The heads will roll, and there will be hell to pay.

Tori just needs to give me the go-ahead.

Chapter 12

Connor

I never imagined our paths would intertwine again, yet it was her heart-wrenching sobs that truly shattered me.

The sound sliced through the serene stillness of the evening—a raw, anguished melody that echoed deep within the recesses of my soul, reverberating with every ounce of pain I had desperately buried over the years.

One day, I hope she can grasp that I walked away from us not out of indifference but to keep her safe, to shield her from the impending storm curdling in my life.

Despite the distance that stretches between us and the years that have slipped by, I have never ceased to think of her—she remains the ghost haunting my thoughts, the specter that dances through my dreams.

Sleepless nights would stretch endlessly, and in those quiet, agonizing hours, my mind would wander back to the image of her face—the way her laughter had once illuminated the room, and the warmth of her touch that enveloped me like a comforting embrace.

I often find myself regretting that fateful day when I chose my father's counsel over my own heart.

If only I had summoned the courage to fight for her, maybe I could have bestowed upon her the life she truly deserved.

She was ready to marry me, her eyes shimmering with unfiltered love and hope, unbowed by the hardships that awaited us.

Yet, the very thought of her enduring struggle by my side gnawed at me; I wanted so much more for her than a life punctuated by financial burdens and uncertainty.

I always understood, deep down, that she had the means to find someone who could care for her as she deserved—a partner capable of honoring her like the goddess she truly was, a radiant being worthy of the world, and more.

And here I am, left to question every decision that has defined my life.

I broke the goddess! I shattered her spirit!

Seeing her curled into a ball of tears feels like a dagger thrust into my heart, each sob resonating with unbearable intensity.

My heart aches, my body is heavy with sorrow, and my very essence feels frail under the weight of this heartache.

Everything else around me fades into insignificance; all I can focus on is the agony I've inflicted upon her and the haunting realization that I might have lost her forever.

Chapter 13

Kass

When I arrived at the airport, Dorian was as prompt as ever.

Haley and Tori are not with him, so I assume he left them at the apartment.

"My Queen, I am glad you made it safe."

We slide into his vehicle, the interior warm and inviting, and begin our journey towards my apartment.

The hum of the engine fills the air as we drive through the familiar streets, the city lights blinking past our windows.

I brace myself for what feels like it might be a lengthy stay, knowing that I'll need to gather my thoughts and energy for whatever awaits.

I roll my eyes, "Maybe one day you will stop with the formality. Give me all the details. What's going on? What happened?"

He sighs, "Tori was at the ball like you suggested. She was having a great time; she even took a man to the library. Turns out she knew that man. The man was CC, who is part of my crew, but that is the ex who broke her heart. She's a mess; she's just huddled in a dark corner, refusing to move or eat. His real name is Connor Chance; I had no idea that he was the ex she mentioned to Hailey. I would have stopped it, I swear!"

"Dorian, you are not at fault! No one knew; I didn't think he could be one of our guys. I reran his background while I was on the jet. They grew up in the same town, dated for eight years, and even filed for a marriage license. They were serious and committed. What did you gather from Conor?"

He looks at me with deep sorrow etched on his face, his sad eyes reflecting a burden he can hardly bear.

"I asked him a few questions, probing gently, and then replayed the audio recording. It's devastating. Apparently, his father disowned him, forcing him to sever all ties with Tori. He was caught in a brutal ultimatum: either abandon Tori or risk having a hit placed on her and her family. In a moment of desperation, Connor accepted the financial incentive from his father, choosing to cut ties not only with his dad but also with Tori, all in a bid to keep her safe from harm. If you look through the file, you'll see the chilling evidence—his father went through with the hit that night. He orchestrated the tragic accident that claimed Tori's parents. He paid off the driver of the eighteen-wheeler, instructing him to follow and collide with their vehicle. What's gut-wrenching is that neither Tori nor Connor is aware of this grim truth; Connor only learned about the death of her parents during our conversation tonight. He is in profound pain, wracked with guilt and grief, especially after Tori confided in him about her own suicide attempt—an act of desperation stemming from the chaos surrounding them. I advised him to go home and promised to meet him shortly. They are both navigating their grief in profoundly different ways, each struggling to cope with the weight of their losses and the secrets that loom over them. I am determined to do everything in my power to help Conor find his way back to a healthier mindset. Can you and Hailey step in to support Tori in the meantime? She will need all the help she can get."

Well shit!

I knew most of it, but their sleeping together again complicates things, at least for Tori.

Tori had just gained her confidence back and Karma had to go and ruin it once again, I am well acquainted with Karma.

I have faced my own battles, but I emerged stronger, discovering the pieces that complete my identity.

To the world outside, I may appear as a frail woman with disabilities, but within the ranks of the Bratva, I am revered as their Queen.

I have a deep compassion for all the women we rescue, nurturing them with my love and strength.

I have learned to protect myself and safeguard my family with unwavering resolve.

I have killed my share of people, but they were either murderers or were trying to harm someone I love.

I take a deep breath.

"Don't worry, Dorian. We can take care of Tori. Hailey and I have been in situations like this before. We will figure this out even if I have to call for backup. Massimo said if you need him or you want to bring Connor up there, our door is always open. I think he could use a visit from you; he is still sulking about Marcus."

Marcus had come to the momentous decision that it was time for him to retire, leaving Massimo feeling a deep sense of personal affront.

The truth beneath it all, however, was rooted in the joy of impending fatherhood—Kiera, his beloved wife, was pregnant with triplets, a true miracle that felt almost unreal.

Doctors had warned them both that she might never have children, a daunting prognosis that weighed heavily on their hearts.

Yet Marcus, fueled by love and determination, had dedicated himself to ensuring her dream of motherhood became a reality.

He took to slipping specially formulated vitamins into her favorite snacks and drinks, nurturing her health in secret, and finally, his unwavering efforts had borne fruit.

With Kiera now on strict bed rest to safeguard both her and the precious lives she carried, Marcus had made the difficult choice to step away from his career entirely. He had resigned a month ago, firmly resolved to remain by her side through every moment of this miraculous journey.

As for Massimo, though the sting of loss hung in the air, he would eventually reconcile with Marcus's choice. He missed his best friend deeply, understanding that sometimes, love and family must take precedence over even the closest of friendships.

As we pull to my apartment, I look at Dorian, "Text me in the morning to let me know how far you got, or if I need to come handle him. Who knows I might give him a piece of my mind anyway! It depends on what Tori has to say. Connor better prepare for the worst, you know what I am capable of!"

"Yes, my Queen"

Let's explore the possibilities of restoration, for, under my reign, not a soul shall fade into the shadows!

Chapter 14

Tori

***B**LACK!*

DARKNESS!

DEATH!

THE WORLD DOESN'T NEED ME.

I NEED TO BE WITH MOM AND DAD.

I NEED THE PAIN TO STOP.

YOU ARE A FAILURE.

YOU DON'T DESERVE TO BE LOVED.

BLACK!

SLIP INTO THE BLACKNESS.

LET THE DARKNESS WIN!

NO ONE NEEDS YOU!

My thoughts are getting the best of me.

Maybe I should go through with it this time.

Hailey has been watching me like a hawk, I can't even breathe without her glancing in my direction.

She just made a peanut butter and jelly sandwich and went wash her hands, she lift the knife on the counter.

GRAB THE KNIFE!

I will—it's time I finally reunite with my mom and dad after all these years.

With a furtive glance, I deftly slide the gleaming knife into the pocket of my jeans, feeling the cool metal press against the fabric.

I rush to the nearest bathroom, heart racing, and swiftly turn the lock, sealing myself away in the cramped space.

It's time.

I am sorry, Mom and Dad; please forgive when you see me.

I am sorry, Connor, I hope you find the love you deserve, and I am glad I won't be here to see you fall in love again.

Conor, you were my first love, and that means everything to me.

I let the tears fall freely; I am done hurting.

I am sorry, Kass. Thank you for saving me for the first time.

Without you, Kass, I would have never found myself and moved on with my life.

I slip the knife out of my pocket. Should I slit my wrists again?

NO!

You're right; there is too much room for error.

The chest is a better place for a kitchen knife to lay.

Goodbye…

Chapter 15

Connor

"What the fuck were you thinking CC? Do you know the damage that you have caused?"

Dorian scolds me with a tone that makes me feel like a wayward child, lost in my own confusion.

"That's the problem, D. I wasn't thinking clearly," I confess, my voice tinged with regret. "I had gone there seeking fun and relaxation, a brief escape from my reality, not to end up tangled in a situation where I'd sleep with anyone, let alone reunite with the love of my life. How is she coping? I can't shake the guilt of knowing I made her cry; it weighs heavily on my heart."

"Stop getting all sentimental on me, CC. But you have to understand, she's really not well. She hasn't eaten in two days and is curled up in a corner of her room, refusing to even look at Hailey. The Queen just arrived and is making her way over now to see what she can do to help. You know you messed with one of the Queen's closest friends, right? You better brace yourself for the worst because Kass doesn't play around when it comes to protecting her girls. There's something I need to share with you that might change the game entirely, okay?"

I take a deep breath as if I thought tonight would get any easier.

"Ok, D. Hit me with it."

"Honestly, I want to hit you since I could be losing my best employee. So, I played the audio back from the library. I heard everything you said about your dad, and you told me a bit more about that. Have you kept track of your dad over the years?"

Weird, why would I do that?

"No, he disowned me, coldly instructing me to never contact him again. I was young and naïve, believing he was one of the most powerful figures in New York, but now I see the truth clearly. He couldn't possibly withstand even half of what we endure. But tell me, why do you ask?"

Dorian sighs, "I know he threatened Tori and her family if you didn't leave. He claimed he would put a hit out, right?"

Yes, where the fuck is this going?

"Dorian, what did you find?"

My heart is beating out of my chest.

What could he have found?

What did Dad do?

Dorian looks at me with sad eyes, "He followed through. He killed Tori's parents soon after you left. He paid the eighteen-wheeler to hit them and make it look like it was an accident. Kass and I looked at it tonight; he never intended to keep his promise. It broke Tori to pieces; luckily, she met Kass and Asia. She was about to kill herself when she met them on her trip to Chicago; that's when Kass gave her the job because we were still in the process of building the club. Kass put Tori back together; she took her in and gave her all the counseling and help she needed, just like she does with all our girls. I don't know what's going to happen with you and Tori, but your dad thinks he can get away with anything. Did you know he's been raping women and laundering money?"

I cannot contain my rage, "You have got to be fucking lying?! The bastard not only killed Tori's family, but he's hurting other women? Dorian, we have got to stop him! What can we do?"

Dorian smirks, "Are you finally ready to get your hands dirty, CC?"

Dorian knows I don't want to get my hands in the not so legal business unless it's necessary, this is one of those times.

"Tell me the plan; he deserves to pay."

"You asked for it, CC! I took a moment to review his associate list, and it turns out we share a few connections. He knows Spencer Peck, a long-time member of our club since its inception. On my way over here, I had a chance to chat with Spencer, and I can tell you, he harbors a deep-seated disdain for your father. However, he tolerates him, as Spencer has a significant stake in your father's company— he holds a whopping fifty percent. It seems your dear old dad found himself buried in debt, and Spencer came to his rescue."

I like where this is going.

"Go on."

"In just three days, Spencer will reach out to your dad to arrange a meeting at Kastaways, which is our designated meeting place. During this time, he will be on our territory and operating under our authority. While he is here, Asia will head up to New York to bring the girls who have been harmed to our secure rescue compound. I know this situation will be challenging for you since it involves your dad, but I need to be clear: he is not going to leave this city. When Spencer arrives, make sure to explain everything to him thoroughly. Spencer has maintained a close friendship with Massimo for many years and is fully aware of our operations, even though he chooses not to get personally involved. You might wonder why that is; it's because Spencer serves as our trusted attorney, providing us with legal guidance whenever necessary. This means we have the opportunity to explore various strategies regarding your dad's company. If you decide that you would like Spencer to take the reins, we can certainly arrange for that to happen. It's important for us to have a solid plan in place, so think carefully about what you want and how to communicate it to Spencer."

"We will show no mercy, just like I'm sure he showed no mercy to those women. You're right. He will not be leaving here. We will consult Spencer to see what we can do with Dad's company, which I don't want. he disowned me, and I don't want any part of his evil Legacy. But I will get my revenge; revenge for those women he hurt, and revenge for Tori.

This is what we do; we remove the evil from the world while making up for it with the good we do.

I will not feel bad about this in any way; it's time for dear old dad to see that he doesn't have as much power as he thinks he does."

Dorian evil smirk is actually quite calming, "You will soon be fully a member of the Bratva. We have always admired what you do for us, but know you are going to fully join our ranks. We will always protect you and always be behind you. We are a family. The only people we can't save you from is Kass and Asia, they scare us. But you will learn quickly. Do you want to take a quick trip with me the Chicago to check on the boss?"

To go see Massimo?

Wow he must trust me even after this whole incident.

"Sure, D. When do we leave?"

His haunting smile reappears, an unsettling reminder of the promise of adventure.

 "Right now! The Queen has graciously lent us her jet. Pack a bag for at least four days."

Four days?

To him, that's merely a brief excursion.

A flicker of anxiety dances in my chest at the
thought of meeting the Don.

I wonder about the tasks that await me—will they
be laborious?

Amidst the excitement, skepticism gnaws at me.

What if my Goddess isn't well? The thought sends
a shiver down my spine.

I am determined to set everything right for her,
even if it means she may never be truly mine again.

Chapter 16

Kass

Nine Days Later….

These past nine days have been the most excruciating of my life.

I arrived just moments too late, my heart pounding with dread as I unlocked the door to my apartment.

The air felt heavy, almost as if it were charged with an unspoken tension.

Rushing to the bathroom, I could hear muffled sounds coming from behind the closed door.

Tori was inside, locked away, clutching the knife she had stealthily taken from the kitchen.

Hailey was doing everything she could to coax her out but I could see the panic on Hailey's because it had been minutes since Tori spoke.

My mind raced with anxiety—how could it have come to this?

Never forget the scene that laid before me.

I've seen people killed and it has never bothered me.

But seeing Tori lying there in a pool of her blood, a knife sticking out of her chest, and her not moving or breathing or responding when I call her name in any way has torn me to pieces.

Really hard to get the image out of my head when you see someone you care about deeply suffering and on the brink of death.

I should have known how bad it was when Dorian called me and said the secret phrase.

Our secret phrase is, "Black is back."

That phrase portrays that dark thoughts have returned, creeping back in like an unwelcome shadow that is so difficult to escape. Some call it "chasing the darkness" or "chasing dark thoughts."

I first encountered these phrases during a deeply insightful counseling workshop I attended, where we delved into the complexities of mental health.

Many veterans refer to these struggles, using language that echoes the battles they've faced both externally and within their own minds.

I've made it a point to educate all my girls about this concept, fostering an environment where we boldly confront our emotions instead of hiding them away.

This approach has been a lifeline for many of the girls we've rescued, a beacon guiding us through difficult times.

But now, for the first time, this philosophy has faltered, and it feels as though my heart is being ripped apart.

As I sit in the cold, sterile chamber of the hospital, the harsh fluorescent lights casting a stark glare on everything around me, I can't help but reflect on my choices and what I might have done differently.

Tori has been fighting for her life for the last six agonizing days, battling against the odds with a strength that both inspires and terrifies me.

I was too late; she had stabbed herself in the abdomen and almost punctured a lung.

From what the doctors said, she tried to stab herself in the heart but must have been rushing and missed.

She absolutely has to pull through this—her strength is something I can't afford to lose.

I need her in my life, and the club depends on her, too.

Tori has become one of my closest friends, a true confidante in a world that often feels overwhelming.

We used to have an open line of communication—a bond that felt unbreakable.

She has been my rock during turbulent times, especially when issues with Massimo crept in.

Tori has this incredible ability to keep me motivated and inspired to strive for more good in the world.

She even makes sure I share a laugh at least once a week, reminding me that joy can often be found amidst the chaos.

How is it possible that someone who brings so much light to others can be suffering so profoundly, hidden from the eyes of those around her?

It's heartbreaking.

From the workshop, I learned that people like Tori, who wear smiles as armor, often wrestle with their own demons in silence.

They do everything within their power to ensure that others find happiness, even at the cost of their own well-being.

If Tori can somehow pull through this ordeal, I promise to devote myself fully to ensuring she never finds herself in such a dark place again.

We've been keeping Tori's struggles hidden from Connor, fearing his reaction.

Dorian mentioned that Connor is improving, and they're addressing the issues surrounding Connor's dad—thank goodness for that.

I know we can't shield him from the truth forever, but the thought of seeing another person I care about hurt or drifting into despair is unbearable.

Massimo has been calling me every day, checking in to ensure I'm managing and seeking updates on Tori's condition.

His intuition about what I need is uncanny.

Tori truly deserves a love that is pure and unwavering—a love that has the power to heal. I can't shake the feeling that Connor is capable of giving her that kind of love.

I truly hope he gets the chance to show her just how much she means to him.

Chapter 17

Connor

Here, I stand behind the one-way window in Kastaways' dungeon.

Usually, the dungeon is reserved for obedience training, but tonight, it's reserved to end a monster.

A creature that never knew the warmth of love, lurking in the shadows of my heart.

A creature ensnared in a web of deceit, orchestrating a symphony of money laundering, hiding its sinister activities behind a mask of charm and charisma.

A monster who thinks consent is not essential.

He is a ruthless titan driven by insatiable greed, willing to go to any lengths to protect his company and accumulate wealth, yet shockingly neglectful of his own son.

A monster who rapes and abuses women.

His tirade ends now!

Spencer lured him here under the pretense that he had reserved a woman to train tonight.

We have been watching him for the last three days; he follows the same routine every day.

He wakes up, goes to work, stalks a woman, assaults a woman, and then goes home to his empty mansion.

Turns out all his household employees quit on him, all because of his actions.

He will never harm another person; he will die by the hand that he cast away.

He slowly enters the dungeon; Cornelis Chance will no longer haunt New York after tonight.

I feel the need rising within me to show him who's more powerful. I hope he hangs on for dear life, and I can drag his end out.

Don't worry, Dad.

I will be a monster like you, but it's only for tonight.

Chapter 18

B<small>EEP</small>.

BEEP.

BEEP.

BEEP.

I recognize a voice, but I can't remember their name.

"I am okay, though I carry a heavy heart. She is beginning to show signs of improvement, which fills me with hope. I promise I will not leave her side during this critical time; she needs my support now more than ever. It's vital for her to understand that she deserves to be loved and cherished and that the world would not be better off without her. Her life is far too precious to lose. If she manages to pull through this, I will dedicatedly show her every single day just how much she means to me. I also believe Connor should come to visit her. Although he has just started on his own path to healing, it's important for him to witness the severity of his actions and the impact they've had on all our lives. It's a hard truth, but facing it might help bring a sense of closure and encourage him to make better choices moving forward."

I can't move; a heavyweight pinions my body to the unforgiving surface beneath me.

I struggle to open my eyes, fighting against the thick darkness that envelops me.

Somewhere in the shadows, I can hear a voice calling out, filled with warmth and urgency, and I long to reach out and touch it, to grasp the source of this lifeline that feels just beyond my reach.

I can't see them, the faces that matter so much to me, but the yearning swells within me—I want to squeeze them tightly and never let them go again.

The thought of their embrace brings a flicker of life to my stillness.

I feel trapped in this twilight realm, where I can hear faint sounds but cannot react; this helplessness gnaws at me, cutting deeper than any physical pain.

Please, God, grant me the strength to pull through this darkness!

I swear I will never find myself in this place again; I have people who love me fiercely, and they need me as much as I need them.

The realization crashes over me like a wave: this time, I will dedicate each day to cherishing every moment, embracing the small joys and connections that fill life with meaning.

I refuse to take any of it for granted again.

Chapter 19

Kass

I am dreading making this phone call, but here goes nothing…

RING.

RING.

RING.

"This is CC; how can I help you?"

What a professional but unusual way to answer the phone.

"Connor, it's Kassani Ballentine. We need to talk. Are you using your Bratva phone?"

He gasps, "Umm, of course, ma'am, what's going on?"

He sounds scared.

GOOD!

HE BETTER FEAR ME!

I take a deep breath, "Tell me everything that happened with your father. Don't leave anything out."

"Yes, ma'am. He arrived at Kastways thinking that Spencer had arranged a woman for him to train, but when he arrived, the dungeon was empty because I was hiding behind the viewing glass. Spencer convinced him to be restrained to the Saint Andrews cross to wait for the woman. That helped me out, and he willingly restrained himself. He started to get angry about being restrained. Spencer put the fear in him before I entered the room. Spencer told him that four days ago, Dad owned nothing. Spencer bought out all of the rest of the shareholders, and apparently, dear old Dad was behind on all the payments for his house and office. Spencer fixed that, too; he bought it all. Dad was only left with the clothes he had and his fancy cars. Dad was screaming and ranting about how he would kill Spencer and whoever helped him. That's when I stepped in. Dad never thought he would see my face again; he went as white as a ghost when I walked in. I told Dad about all the things he missed: my accomplishments, my struggles, and meeting Tori again."

Connor's voice saddened as he said her name, "Continue, I need to know everything."

I maintained a commanding tone in my voice, ensuring that he could sense the weight of my authority, a reminder of the power I held at that moment.

He gathers himself according to his tone, "It took him several moments to realize who I was. That tells you how much he didn't care to keep track of my life. I told him that this was the place where he would die for all the crimes that he committed against all those women. I wasn't worried about what he did to me, but I was worried about what he did to Tori's family and all of the other women that he harmed."

"How did you do it? How did you end his life?"

"Definitely not my proudest moment, but I found out what he had been doing to all those women. he would mark them with his initials, brand them with a CC, and would then rape them. So, I carved TC into his chest for Tori, and then I took the biggest butt plug I could find and shoved it down his throat. I asked him how it felt when consent was ignored. To finish him off, I stabbed him in the heart and twisted the knife around until he stopped screaming. It brought me peace knowing he would not harm another soul. I told Spencer to do whatever he desired with Dad's company, but I wanted no part of it. Spencer gave me $2 billion dollars because he said that I deserved to be able to not work as hard. The company is being sold off bit by bit, so Spencer gets back all he put in. He is buried where Dorian told me to bury him; he will never harm anyone again."

I am a little surprised he followed through, when it comes to family paying for their crimes it can be a gray area.

"How did that make you feel, Connor?"

I need him to let all the anger out before I bring up Tori.

He sighs, "I am no longer angry, I'm hurt that after all these years he never changed his ways. But I am glad he can't hurt anyone anymore."

I am glad he's working through this; I am dreading telling.

"I am glad you worked out your emotions. What are you doing right now?"

"I just got to my office; why?"

I take a deep breath, "Sit down and listen carefully."

Chapter 20

Connor

What could Kassani possibly have to share with me that's so important?

I take a deep breath and slowly lower myself into my throne, the imposing centerpiece of my office.

Its grandeur and scale dominate the space, a symbol of authority and power, and as I sink into its embrace, I can't help but feel the weight of expectation that comes with it.

I set the phone down on my desk and put it on speaker.

"Okay, ma'am. What's going on?"

She lets out the breath she's holding, "We were letting you heal, so we didn't tell you, but you need to know."

"Spit it out, ma.' am I have got work to do."

She huffs, "Learn some patience! Tori is getting better, but she is still in the hospital."

WHAT??

"Who put her in the hospital? What exactly happened? Who do I need to hunt down for this? I refuse to lose her again!"

"Connor, please, you need to calm down. Just make sure you're still seated. She's been in a coma for nearly a week now."

ARE YOU SERIOUS?!

I take a deep breath, forcing myself to steady my racing heart. "Ma'am, please tell me everything that happened. Tori has always been my greatest weakness, my anchor in this chaotic world. I need to know the truth—don't hold anything back!"

"This is going to be tough to hear. But that night after the ball, Tori was a complete train wreck. I sent Hailey over to be with her, but I didn't arrive soon enough to prevent what happened next. I could still hear Tori's sobs echoing in my mind when Dorian called me and the emptiness in her eyes when I finally found her. I can't shake the feeling that I could have made a difference if I had left sooner. It's been haunting me ever since."

"Kassani, tell me. Say it."

She takes another deep breath, "She tried to kill herself again. She had been here in the hospital because I found her locked in the bathroom in a pool of her own blood. She wasn't breathing, and her body was starting to go cold."

WHAT!!!

"No, you're lying! Who really hurt her?"

NO!

NO!

"Connor, we're uncertain about what triggered this episode. She experienced something similar once before; that's when I first crossed paths with her. At that time, we managed to intervene before she could inflict any serious harm on herself. But this time, it seems I arrived too late. Nevertheless, it's crucial that we remain by her side as she navigates through this challenging storm. If you feel ready, I invite you to join me at the hospital; she could really use the support."

"I am on my way. I will not leave her side."

"Thank you, Connor. I hope you get your second chance."

Me too.

Goddess, you mustn't leave me!

The thought of losing you fills me with a despair I can't bear.

You are my reason for being the light in my darkest hours.

You are my chance, my beacon of hope amid the chaos.

You are my Tore, the embodiment of all that is beautiful and pure in this world.

You are my one true love, the bond that holds my heart captive.

I need you more than words can express.

Without you, my existence feels hollow, devoid of joy and purpose.

Pull through!

From this moment on, I vow never to leave your side again!

You may love me or hate me, but always remember, you are forever mine.

Chapter 21

BEEP.

BEEP.

BEEP.

BEEP.

The beeps in my dreams need to leave!

Every time I hear a beep, I see the one thing I don't want to see in my dreams.

Connor.

CC.

Whoever the fuck he is now!

It's as if my heart is nudging me to forgive him and move on, yet the little devil perched on my shoulder keeps whispering that I'm too fat for someone like Connor, a model whose very presence seems to shine.

I can't help but think back to the days when I felt confident in my own skin before the weight crept in.

Maybe that's why, at the ball, he didn't even recognize me when we were being intimate.

Now, the voice returns, but this time, it feels enveloped by something—a warmth, perhaps.

"I am so glad you came."

That familiar voice, resonating with sincerity, wraps around me like a comforting blanket. It feels as though this voice genuinely cares, lifting me from the shadows of self-doubt.

"I wish you would've told me sooner."

THAT VOICE!

The way it resonates makes me tremble, stirring something deep within me.

I yearn to break free from the darkness that has clung to me for so long.

If only I could reach out through this emotional haze and connect with that sad, raspy voice, bridging the distance between us.

If only I could grasp his hand and pull him into my world!

I find myself yearning to break free from this chaotic world that binds me as the voices call out with an urgent need for connection.

They resonate within me like a longing to be enveloped in the warmth of a long, comforting embrace, where the weight of the world can momentarily be lifted and solace can be found.

This enveloping darkness must fade away; I yearn to step into the radiant light.

I long to illuminate the world around me!

Chapter 22

Connor

Three Weeks Later..

"I just wanted to let you know," I tell Kassani over a video message, my voice tinged with concern. "She's been shifting and twitching, but she hasn't fully woken up yet."

Kassani had to rush back home after an incident arose—Massimo urgently needed her assistance with one of the girls. Despite the distance, she makes a point to check in every day, her guilt evident in her anxious expression as she glances at the screen.

"She needs to wake up soon; what are the doctors saying?"

I sigh, "They say that her brain activity is almost normal, and her heart rhythm is stable. But they think the reason she's not waking up is due to the mental toll all the events of her life put on her."

"We are no giving up hope! She will wake up! Have you been talking to her everyday like they suggested?"

I looked at Kass with pleading eyes, my heart racing as I struggled to articulate my thoughts. "Kass, you know how hard it is for me to express my emotions, especially when it comes to telling Tore everything that's weighing on my heart. Do you really think talking to her might help bring her back to us?"

Kass's lips curled into a warm smile, and I could see the understanding in her eyes.

"First, I'm really glad you're comfortable enough with me to stop calling me ma'am!"

She laughed lightly, easing the tension in the room.

"Second, the human body and mind work in mysterious ways. What might work for one person won't necessarily resonate with another; it's all part of a trial-and-error process. It can't hurt to speak your truth to her. In fact, it might just be the spark she needs. Just give it a try! She needs us now more than ever! We are all she has, and we will not give up on her!"

Her words ignited a flicker of hope within me, reminding me of the bond we shared and the strength we could muster together.

"Okay, ma'am! I will keep you updated. I will try, I promise. I need my chance to make this right."

"Thanks, CC! We will get through this! I will call you again soon."

I simply nod and end the video call, a heaviness settling over my shoulders as I exhale slowly.

Can the Goddess truly hear the silent pleas of my heart?

Should I bravely expose the depths of my soul to her, revealing my most profound fears and deepest longings?

The burden of unspoken words weighs heavily on my heart; each thought is a flicker of vulnerability just waiting to be unleashed.

Will she ever find her way back to me, or have I irrevocably lost her to the sands of time and fate?

The uncertainty gnaws at me, casting shadows over my thoughts, making every moment feel like an eternity.

Tore awakens in me a sense of poetic wonder, igniting a feeling within that everything I do is laced with yearning and emotional depth. Each glance, each shared silence, seems infused with meaning, as if the universe conspires to intertwine our destinies once more.

I haven't felt this alive in years—this ache for connection and understanding—ever since I made the heart-wrenching decision to leave her.

The memory of what we once shared lingers in the air like sweet incense, haunting yet beautiful, reminding me of everything I left behind.

I take a deep breath, "Tore, do you remember our first kiss?"

Chapter 23

This dream feels all too real…

"We have been dating for six months! You let me hold your hand and hug you, but there's something else I want."

What could this voice want?

This voice has a face that seems like I know it, and it should be important to me, but I can't place it!

This world that I am stuck in infuriates me!

"What else could you want? I am a very sensible girl, but I am not into foolish things!"

The voice chuckles, "Tore, I am not asking for what you're thinking."

The voice calls me Tore; why do I like that so much?

"And what am I thinking, mister? Since you think you know me so well!"

The voice chuckles softly, a playful lilt to its tone, "Your mind went straight to desire because that's all anyone at our high school seems to think about. I admit, I ponder it sometimes, but deep down, I know we're not truly ready. Yet, I do crave something sweet."

As the voice tenderly caressed my face, a warm tingle surged through me, igniting a spark I didn't know I had.

"What exactly is this sweet thing you're after? Strawberries, perhaps?" I ventured, my heart racing.

With a charming grin, the voice wrapped its arms around my waist, drawing me closer. "I bet your lips are sweeter than any strawberries. May I kiss you, Tore?"

Why does my heart flutter with nervous excitement?

Why am I so desperate to discover the taste of those lips?

"Yes, please, kiss me." The words fell from my lips, trembling with anticipation.

The voice pulled me in tighter, its arms encircling me like a fortress, offering comfort and a sense of belonging.

I felt the gentle tilt of its head as those soft, luscious lips moved toward mine, almost in slow motion.

When our mouths finally met, it was like igniting an instant blaze—an explosion of sweetness and longing.

At that moment, everything shifted; I realized too late that there was no going back.

Those lips had forever altered the landscape of my heart, leaving me achingly aware and irrevocably drawn to them, rendered unable to be pleased by anyone else's desire!

This voice has captured my soul.

Chapter 24

Connor

I gently caress Tore's forehead, feeling the warmth of her skin beneath my fingertips.

"I'll never forget that day, Tore. The moment our lips met for the first time, I knew in my heart that you were my forever. I'm truly sorry for everything that I've done in the past. I know the pain about your family weighs heavily on you, but you don't need to worry anymore. I made sure the person responsible faced justice; they would never harm another family or woman again.
The family you have now—though it may look different than what you imagined—will always stand by your side. You have me, Kass, and the entire Bratva, who are all fiercely loyal and ready to support you. No matter what life throws our way, we will be right by your side, helping you navigate through it all. You're not allowed to walk away from us; you mean more to us than you can possibly know. My life would be unrecognizable without you, and I shudder to think of where I would be without your light. We may have started as kids, lost in our innocent love, but now we stand as adults, unburdened by the judgments of those who once loomed over us. This is our time—please, pull through for me and for our love. We deserve our chance at happiness; we deserve to be whole, not torn or broken. Let me love you forever and always."

Can she truly hear me?

I doubt it; if she could, it would be nothing short of a miracle.

The stillness around us feels almost palpable, as if the very air is holding its breath, waiting for a response that may never come.

My right hand gently rests on the cool, sterile surface of her hospital bed while my left fingers glide over the screen of my phone, lost in a sea of notifications.

Suddenly, I feel a light pressure enveloping my hand.

Startled, I look up and meet her gaze.

Tore's eyes, usually vibrant, are filled with a mix of exhaustion and determination.

She lets out a weary sigh and whispers, "Water."

"Goddess, I will get the doctor," I reply, a rush of relief flooding through me at the sight of her wakefulness. "I'm so glad you're awake."

Mine.

I will not screw this up!

Chapter 25

Three weeks after leaving the hospital…

Since leaving the hospital, my perspective on life has been profoundly transformed.

I've come to realize just how many people genuinely care about my well-being.

Kass reaches out to me every week, her voice tinged with concern.

I can sense that she carries a weight of guilt, but I remind myself that my mental health isn't a burden she should feel responsible for.

The one person I see every day is the one person I held a grudge against for too many years.

CC.

Connor Chance is the man who proves that love is something truly special.

Love is the quiet patience of understanding during tough times, a steady presence that reassures you it's okay to be vulnerable.

Love is the surprise of random flowers, their vibrant colors brightening a mundane Tuesday, a gentle reminder that beauty can exist in unexpected places.

Love is savoring sushi on a casual Wednesday night, laughter echoing as you share your favorite rolls and discuss the little joys of life.

Love is the warmth of a freshly brewed cup of coffee brought to me in bed, allowing hours to slip away as I immerse myself in a good book, lost in thought until the early hours of the morning.

Love is the safety felt while falling asleep, his arms wrapped tightly around me, creating a cocoon of comfort that keeps the world outside at bay.

Love is the commitment to never go to bed angry, always choosing to communicate openly and resolve conflicts, and ensuring peace reigns in our hearts.

Love is the willingness to dive deep into meaningful conversations about our feelings, sharing hopes, fears, and dreams without hesitation.

Love is the understanding and support for each other's mental health, recognizing when to lend a listening ear or offer a moment of solace.

Love is nurturing a relationship with oneself, embracing imperfections, and learning to celebrate who you are, unfiltered and genuine.

Love is the profound acknowledgment that each person matters, their thoughts and feelings valued, fostering a sense of belonging.

Love is the self-awareness to recognize how you feel and the courage to express those feelings, creating a foundation of trust and authenticity.

Love is rolling over in the soft, warm sheets of your bed and gently kissing the man who has steadfastly chosen to remain by your side through all of life's ups and downs.

Love is mustering the courage to seek help by going to therapy, understanding that vulnerability is a strength, and embracing the journey toward healing and self-discovery.

Love is the gradual return of joy, expressed in the heartfelt smiles that break through the clouds of despair, reminding you that happiness is not just a distant memory but a vibrant possibility once again.

The journey of healing after my attempt to end my life has been a long and arduous path, but at last, I feel a glimmer of my true self returning.

Today is a significant day—a milestone of sorts.

Today marks the moment Dorian has finally agreed to welcome me back to work.

I can hardly contain my excitement at the prospect of stepping behind the bar again!

I'm eager to mix, stir, and create moments of joy for all the hopeful souls who find their way to Kastaways.

The name "Kastaways" has taken on a profound significance for me.

Kass shared her vision behind the name, revealing that it represents a sanctuary—a safe haven for anyone who feels different or judged.

It's designed to be a home, a shelter, and a beacon of hope.

Everyone who walks through its doors is embraced, regardless of their appearance, taste, or preferences.

As you enter, the main floor greets you with the vibrant energy of a classic club scene, while the underground second floor exudes an aura of exclusivity, an elite retreat.

Without the tattoo or the membership fee, entry to this hidden realm is simply not permitted.

The third floor, the once-bustling dungeon of training, is now closed off; no sessions will be held until Dorian decides otherwise.

I should start preparing myself; I have a strong feeling that an undeniably attractive man will be perched at the bar tonight, waiting for a captivating conversation.

Chapter 26

Spencer Peck

These last three months have worn me down.

As an attorney representing the Bratva, my life is a whirlwind of travel, constantly shuttling between my home base and the bustling streets of Chicago whenever my expertise is required.

Each trip is a blend of anticipation and responsibility as I navigate the complexities of the legal world intertwined with the shadowy dealings of organized crime.

Tonight, I need to relax.

So, head to the one place I tend to visit anytime I am in town: Kastaways.

It has been nearly eight years since I last found myself in a relationship.

The ending of that chapter was marked by a painful betrayal—Cornelius Chance, someone I once trusted, chose to pursue her for himself.

His actions were far from gracious, and though he treated her poorly, she believed that the grass was greener on his side of the fence.

That decision shattered what we had, leaving behind lingering questions and a bittersweet sense of loss.

The worst part is she was his decoy to be able to rape other women.

I didn't hesitate when the Bratva, the notorious crime syndicate, asked for my help in taking down Cornelius Chance.

After all, he was a ruthless businessman whose deceitful practices had left many in ruin.

The way he exploited the vulnerable and manipulated the system had not only enraged the Bratva, but it had crossed every moral line in the book.

I knew he deserved everything that CC did to him— retribution that finally put an end to his reign of terror.

I came to Mississippi in the middle of Mardi Gras season, and months later, I am still here.

I know I will have to trek back to Chicago eventually, but right now, I need time for me.

The atmosphere of Kastaways always wraps around me like a warm blanket, soothing my restless spirit.

The soft glow of the pendant lights casts a gentle luminescence, creating cozy shadows that flicker against the walls, and the low murmur of laughter and clinking glasses fills the air, underscoring the evening's conviviality.

As I step onto the top floor, I quickly realize it's the perfect space for mixing and mingling; however, it feels strangely unfamiliar tonight.

The vibrant crowd is filled with faces I don't recognize, each engrossed in their own conversations and laughter, leaving me to float among them like a whisper lost in the wind.

Descending to the second floor, I'm greeted by a familiar sense of belonging.

This is my sanctuary, my safe space. The subtle scents of gourmet food waft through the air, wrapping around me like an embrace, and the sound of a soft jazz band playing in the corner lulls me further into comfort.

This is where I can truly be myself, away from the chaos above.

I take a deep breath as I travel down in the elevator, hoping that tonight will provide a brief respite from recent trials and tribulations.

I remind myself of my purpose for being here, the rejuvenating hope that flickers within me.

I came here to see her—to check in on her well-being, to understand her better, to uncover the layers of her vibrant personality.

I want to experience the unique flavors of her creations, crafted with love and passion.

More than anything, I'm striving for that elusive moment of peace, a chance to quiet my racing mind and ease my troubled heart in her presence.

Maybe she will notice me, maybe I can see where we can go.

Chapter 27

Kastways is buzzing with energy tonight, an unexpected sight for a Monday when one might expect the place to be nearly deserted.

I find myself here not simply because Dorian urged me to come but because I genuinely worry that my Goddess might push herself too hard.

I am filled with pride as I watch her thrive in her recovery; she's become so open with me, revealing her newfound sense of self-worth like a blooming flower, vibrant and full of life.

Dorian has me making rounds throughout the crowded bar, ensuring everything runs smoothly.

I know his true motive, though—he wants to keep me from sitting at the bar, lost in thought as I watch Tore, afraid I'll inadvertently scare off her customers with my lingering gaze.

As I make my way back over to the bar, my gaze catches the striking figure of the Goddess, her eyes filled with curiosity as they lock onto mine.

As I approach, the murmur of conversation fades, and I hear her voice—a melody laced with recognition.

"I have heard your voice before. Did you come to visit me in the hospital?"

I pause for a moment, puzzled by her inquiry. Who could she possibly be talking to?

The silhouette of the person beside her feels oddly familiar.

Oh!

It's Spencer.

The realization comes over me like a warm wave, and I quickly step up to the bar, resting my palms on the polished wood that gleams under the low light.

Her question hangs in the air, but the moment she spots me, all thoughts of it seem to vanish.

"Hey, Chance! Want me to make you my signature drink? I just gave one to this gentleman here," she says, her smile illuminating her face.

She gestures animatedly towards Spencer, who looks a little surprised but pleased.

Tore is back to calling me 'Chance'—her playful nickname for me—and it sends a delightful flutter through my chest, making my heart swell with warmth.

The way she says it feels like an inside joke just between us, a bond reignited in this lively bar atmosphere.

"Sure, my love! Yes, Spencer came to visit you when you were in the hospital. He helped me get the courage to talk to you while you were in the coma, between him and Kass I was never allowed to stop talking to you. He told you some stories and even told you how safe you were. He will officially be one of us tonight if he accepts."

Spencer looks at me with emotional eyes, "Is that why you and Dorian insisted I come tonight?"

I put my hand on his shoulder, "Yes, Dorian got the go-ahead from Massimo. If you want the tattoo and full protection, it's yours."

Spencer smiles, "I guess it's only fitting since Massimo is a big part of my career."

"Good! We can't wait to make you are brother. The ceremony will be tonight after work, as long as Goddess is not tired she will be there too."

Spencer glances at Tore with longing and compassion. Could there be some feelings there?

Would I be ok with that?

With Spencer, yes!

I would do anything for her.

Recently, I've been thinking about how deeply I care for Tore.

Her willingness to explore new dimensions in our relationship has opened up a lot of possibilities.

She approached me the other night with a surprising request: she asked me to consider bringing another partner into our dynamic.

At first, I felt a wave of sadness wash over me as if my love alone couldn't fulfill her needs. It made me question our bond and whether I was enough for her.

However, after I voiced my feelings, Tore took the time to explain her thought process.

She shared her belief that love can expand and that having another partner could enrich our experiences together rather than detract from what we have.

I could sense her sincerity, and it made me rethink my initial reaction.

I plan to talk to Spencer soon to see if he would be interested in joining our relationship.

He's someone I trust, and I think he could bring a new perspective to our journey.

It's a lot to process, but I'm willing to explore this path with Tore, as long as it strengthens the connection we share.

Do I find men attractive?

Yes and no.

I can appreciate that men possess their own unique forms of attractiveness—whether it's their confidence, sense of humor, or physical appearance.

However, I've never been in a romantic relationship with a man or explored that dynamic in my life.

My experiences and attractions have always leaned in a different direction, but I acknowledge the appeal of men within that broader context.

If that's what my Goddess wants, I will follow her direction.

Chapter 28

Weeks Earlier...

The sterile, clinical smell of the hospital hits me like a heavy weight every single time I walk through those dreaded automatic doors.

I've always hated hospitals.

That day, I was sitting in Connor's office, buried in documents and preparing to dive into the details of his father's intricate contract, when his phone rang. It was the call that would change everything—Tori had attempted to take her own life.

Connor is the kind of person who wears his heart on his sleeve, so when he receives the news, he doesn't hesitate to press the speaker button, allowing me to hear every agonizing word from Kass.

The tension in the room was suffocating. Connor's face flashed with raw emotion, a turmoil of guilt and fear consuming him.

At that moment, I wished I could erase his blame; it was not his fault, not in any way.

My first visit to this sterile sanctum came on the heels of Connor's call, a wave of dread washing over me.

Witnessing someone you care about in such a fragile state shatters your heart into countless pieces.

Tori had always been a bright light, her infectious laughter and radiant smile capable of lighting up even the darkest corners of a room.

Now, however, as I stepped into her dimly lit hospital room, her stillness was a harsh contrast to the vibrant spirit I had come to know and admire.

Her delicate frame lay motionless, the rhythmic sound of the beeping machines serving as a grim reminder of her dire condition.

Looking at her serene but pale face, I was struck by a sudden surge of gratitude for my own life, regardless of the mundane worries I often took for granted. It was alarming how quickly circumstances could shift, throwing someone into a personal battle with their own mind.

This moment ignited a fierce desire in me to support anyone struggling with their mental health, to offer understanding and compassion to those like Tori, who face unimaginable challenges every day.

Despite the scars that life has left on her, Tori remains breathtakingly beautiful, her spirit more captivating than any physical attribute.

I've noticed she doesn't fit the conventional mold of beauty, but honestly, her heart radiates warmth, unlike anything I've ever seen. Over the times I've been to the club, I've found myself attracted to her essence, drawn to the kindness she exudes.

I wonder if there's a chance, I could pursue something meaningful with her in the future. And if not Tori, someone with a spirit equal to hers—a light in a world that sometimes feels overwhelmingly dark.

In my time here, I learned that Tori and Connor were high school sweethearts, a love story that started with innocence and has been tested by the harsh realities of life.

Connor often shares his hope that they can rekindle their love once Tori emerges from this darkness. It's clear he thinks no one could ever hold a candle to her.

Despite the women he has dated, his heart seems to continually drift back to the memories of the moments they shared—the laughter, the adventures, and the simple yet profound affection they had for each other.

I crave that sense of connection—the kind that makes life feel rich and significant. I let out a gentle sigh, the weight of my thoughts pressing down on me as I leaned closer to her.

"Hi, Tori. It's Spence," I say softly, the words spilling from my heart. "I truly hope you're finding some peace amidst this chaos and allowing both your mind and body to heal. So many people care deeply about you and are here to support you through this. Connor loves you more than anything in the world; I can see the depth of his affection and the depths of his pain in these past few days. Personally, I wish to express my fondness for you as well; you truly have a spirit that I could genuinely love or find in others. You are such a vibrant soul— deserving to be cherished and protected. I long for the day I see that bright, radiant smile again; it has a remarkable ability to illuminate even the darkest moments. You have this incredible knack for uttering exactly what we need to hear when we're feeling the weight of the world on our shoulders. Please remember to remain true to yourself; your essence is perfect just as it is. Connor often calls you a Goddess, and that title suits you beautifully. When I look at you, I see a strong, resilient woman who, despite the overwhelming challenges, needs a solid support system behind her. I have complete faith that when you come through this tough period, you'll find an unwavering foundation of love and encouragement standing steadfastly by your side. Just know that you truly deserve the world, and I'm here, standing ready to help you reach it."

Everyone deserves to thrive in this world, not just exist.

Chapter 29

Present Day

My first day back at work was utterly exhausting; who would have guessed that a Monday night could be so hectic?

The pace was relentless as I expertly managed to serve over 350 drinks, each one crafted with care in the midst of the bustling crowd.

Surprisingly, I only took two food orders amidst the chaos, highlighting just how focused the night was on the vibrant energy of drink orders flying in from all directions.

Even though I'm completely exhausted from the long day, I've decided to stay late to witness the ceremony for Spencer.

Tonight is a significant milestone for him as he officially becomes a part of the Bratva.

Although he has been working closely with them for years in his role as their attorney, tonight marks a pivotal moment; he isn't just their lawyer anymore—he is being welcomed as a brother into their brotherhood.

The atmosphere is thick with anticipation, and I can feel the weight of the occasion as friends and allies gather to celebrate this meaningful transition in Spencer's life.

It's currently 3:15 a.m.

The club, with its dim lighting and pulsating music, has only been closed for a brief 15 minutes. Yet, everyone here knows our strict policy; they are always out by three on the dot as if adhering to an unwritten law.

Massimo and Kass made a special trip for this ceremony, highlighting the importance of tonight's gathering.

The room buzzes with energy as the thirty-five attendees, all members of the Bratva, share quiet laughter and hushed conversations while I stand slightly apart, an outsider among this tightly-knit circle.

Aside from me, everyone carries an air of authority and loyalty, their tattooed arms and sharp suits broadcasting stories only they know. But despite my outsider status, I received a personal invitation. Kass, Connor, and even Spencer, with his signature grin, ensured I understood how much they wanted my presence here.

I guess it's a perk of dating one of the Bratva members—being allowed to witness the intricate dance of power and tradition that unfolds within these walls.

All of the Bratva members share quiet laughter and hushed conversations while I stand slightly apart, an outsider among this tightly-knit circle.

Aside from me, everyone carries an air of authority and loyalty, their tattooed arms and sharp suits broadcasting stories only they know. But despite my outsider status, I received a personal invitation. Kass, Connor, and even Spencer, with his signature grin, ensured I understood how much they wanted my presence here.

I guess it's a perk of dating one of the Bratva members—being allowed to witness the intricate dance of power and tradition that unfolds within these walls.

Massimo's voice pierces the silence of the room, commanding attention as the atmosphere shifts with palpable anticipation.

"This moment has been a long time coming!" he declares, his tone resonating with a mixture of pride and gravity. "Spencer has stood by my side from the very beginning; now, we can finally honor him as one of our own. He deserves our utmost respect, having saved both my life and the lives of many others time and time again. Our Bratva is deeply grateful for everything you've done, Spencer. Tonight, you will receive your Bratva heart tattooed in a place of your choosing. Once that ink sets into your skin, you will be one of us until your last breath. We will stand by you and your chosen partner for all eternity. Spencer Peck, are you ready to pledge your life to us?"

With a steady nod, Spencer replies, "Until I can protect and punish no more."

There's something undeniably magnetic about his words.

"Who will you choose to ink your skin? You may select up to two people."

"I choose you, M, and Connor. You both are the greatest reasons I stand here today. My loyalty will endure forever."

Connor steps forward, his expression serious yet reassuring, as he picks up the tattoo gun.

"You need never worry again because your brothers, sisters, and wives will cherish and safeguard you until your final breath."

As Connor finishes his statement, his gaze lingers on me, igniting a flicker of curiosity and warmth within.

From my vantage point, I watch as Connor meticulously traces the heart stencil onto Spencer's skin before beginning the tattoo.

Then, with precise strokes, Massimo completes the design by adding the majestic crown above the heart.

This ritual symbolizes a profound bond of love and unwavering protection, and it strikes a chord deep within me, a poignant reminder of the strength found within this brotherhood.

Massimo commands the room with an air of authority, his voice resonating as he announces, "Tonight is a celebration of Spencer, but since he expressed his desire to avoid the spotlight, I have two important announcements to make." He pauses, scanning the gathered crowd, before continuing. "First, as many of you know, I am in need of a new second-in-command. There's truly only one option for this vital position. Dorian, if you're ready to travel or relocate once again, will you step up and be my second?"

Dorian glances at his wife, Hailey, seated nearby, seeking her approval.

She nods encouragingly; her eyes filled with pride.

With a determined look, Dorian replies, "Only if my wife and I are allowed to move back to Chicago."

A wave of surprise washes over the room. The thought of Dorian leaving means no more Hailey at the club.

Their presence has become integral, and now a question lingers in the air: Who will manage the club in their absence?

Massimo smirks, a knowing glint in his eye. "Done. Kass, my Queen, you will have the opportunity to decide what you want to do with the club moving forward."

His tone conveys a mix of confidence and respect.

"Now for my second order of business," he continues, his expression shifting to one of seriousness. "With Dorian returning home, I need to appoint a commander for this area. I've carefully considered my options and Connor; Gulfport is yours if you want it."

Connor's gaze darts toward me, a spark of ambition igniting in his eyes. "Yes, Pakhan. I will serve you well."

A smile spreads across his face, and I can't help but note the weight of his words—he just referred to Massimo as "Pakhan"!

Massimo's eyes narrow playfully at Connor's enthusiasm, and I stifle a giggle at the tone of their exchange.

In a mock show of intimidation, Massimo punches Connor lightly on the shoulder.

"Call me that again, and you'll regret it! Everyone knows I despise that level of formality. I don't answer to Don or Pakhan, and only one person gets away with calling me different nicknames."

At this, Kass's cheeks flush bright red as she attempts to hide behind Massimo, her embarrassment endearing.

The love and camaraderie shared between them fills me with hope and joy, a reminder of the bonds forged within this tightly-knit circle.

Chapter 30

Kass

One week later...

I've found myself stalling lately, caught up in a whirlwind of emotions and responsibilities.

To distract myself, I've been dedicating additional time to Tori, supporting her as she navigates the challenges ahead. I've also been helping Hailey prepare for her next chapter, assisting her with packing up her things and reflecting on the shifts in our lives.

Hailey and I have both come to an understanding: if she desires it, the club, Kastaways, should rightfully belong to Tori.

This decision isn't easy, and we want to ensure it's something Tori genuinely wants, so we're offering her a choice. She can take the reins as the manager of Kastaways, focusing on making it a vibrant hub in our community, or she can step into the more complex world of the Bratva and own the club fully, gaining a deeper connection to our legacy and responsibilities.

Ultimately, it's crucial that whatever path Tori chooses aligns with her strengths and capabilities.

We want this to be her decision, one that empowers her rather than overwhelms her.

To help her relax and reflect on the options ahead, I'm taking her to the spa where we first met— a place that symbolizes renewal and connection for both of us.

Tori is one of the strongest women I know; her resilience and determination inspire me daily.

She deserves not just to survive but to truly thrive in whatever role she embraces.

My hope is that she will choose to become a sister in the Bratva, forging a legacy that she can be proud of.

Chapter 31

It's like Kass intuitively knows exactly what I need at this moment.

She invited me to a spa day—a much-needed escape after the chaos of the last few months.

The thought of soothing massages, calming scents, and peaceful ambiance feels like a balm for my weary soul.

Kass has been an unwavering presence in my life, checking on me constantly and making sure I feel supported.

Her encouragement has become a cornerstone of my recovery, reminding me that I'm not alone on this journey.

Following her recommendation, I started seeing the counselor she suggested.

I can genuinely feel a shift within myself as I've begun to open up more about my feelings.

Each session feels like a step closer to unpacking the heaviness I've been carrying.

The persistent blackness that clouded my mind has finally begun to lift.

I've noticed a significant reduction in my negative thoughts lately, and I attribute part of this progress to the medication I'm now taking to help stabilize my emotions.

It's a relief to feel a sense of balance returning to my life.

My two biggest supporters throughout all of this have been Kass and Connor.

Their encouragement has been invaluable.

Recently, Spencer has also stepped up, checking in on me every day without fail.

He's gone above and beyond, dropping off comforting meals and cheerful bouquets, and has taken the time to settle in for movie nights with me and Connor.

While Spencer has a playful flirtation about him, he's always respectful of the bond that Connor and I share.

His lightheartedness brings a fun energy that adds a bit of joy to the otherwise heavy moments, and I truly appreciate his ability to uplift without crossing any boundaries.

Connor and I have had several conversations about the possibility of expanding our relationship to include another person.

We've been exploring the idea of inviting someone who shares our values and interests. One name that keeps coming up in our discussions is Spencer.

We both feel a connection with him and believe he might complement our dynamic.

It's an exciting prospect, but we want to ensure that we approach it thoughtfully and with open communication.

This foot massage is everything I hoped for and more!

The soothing pressure applied to my arches felt like a gentle wave of relief, melting away the tension accumulated from a long day.

The warm oils used were infused with calming lavender, creating a relaxing aroma that enveloped the room.

Each stroke was expertly crafted, targeting the reflex points on my soles, which not only eased my aching feet but also left me feeling rejuvenated and balanced.

I emerged from the experience with a deep sense of tranquility and renewed energy, truly surpassing all my expectations!

As I settle into the plush chair, I admire my freshly painted violet toes and the elegant acrylic fingernails that adorn my hands.

The soft music envelops the room, drowning out the outside world and readying me for pure relaxation.

"Do you have an ulterior motive for inviting me to the spa, Kass?" I ask, arching an eyebrow playfully.

She grins a spark of mischief in her eyes. "I'm not as worried about you as I was before, but I still plan on checking in every week, if not every day. And yes, I do have a reason for inviting you here. I'll spill the details as soon as we're at the restaurant."

What in the world could she want to share?

"Alright, Kass, just so you know, I'm paying for this appointment. No arguing," I declare, feigning seriousness.

She bursts into laughter, a sound so infectious that it lightens my heart. "Nice try! I prepaid!"

Naturally, she did!

"You win this round, Kass. But just know, I love you."

Chapter 32

As we step into the restaurant, a whirlwind of nerves courses through me, causing my hands to tremble slightly.

What if Tori doesn't want to be part of our sisterhood?

What if her heart remains set on managing Kastaways instead?

Will she choose to embrace the bond of our sisterhood and join us?

I remember the glimmer in her eyes at Spencer's ceremony; it was as if she was weighing the significance of aligning herself with the hope and tradition woven into the fabric of the Bratva.

As women, we are held to a different standard.

While we aren't expected to engage in violence unless we choose to, our roles are crucial in navigating the legal complexities that surround the Bratva.

I oversee the shelter alongside Asia, where we provide refuge for the women we've rescued from the horrors of trafficking.

Hailey and Asia defy convention, seamlessly straddling both the men's and women's Bratva; their unique positions mark them as exceptions to every rule.

They are not just members; they are our most valuable assets.

The waitress, with her dark hair tied back in a neat bun, glides over to our secluded booth at the back of the dimly lit restaurant, her notepad poised for our order.

The ambient sounds of sizzling grills and soft music create a warm atmosphere.

We decide to go for the sushi platter, a colorful array of fresh rolls, nigiri, and sashimi, and each order two icy sodas to accompany it.

"Spill, Kass!" She urges, leaning forward with curiosity etched across her face. "What's all this about? I know you're heading back to Chicago, but there's definitely more to it, isn't there?"

My heart races as I gather my thoughts.

Tori is a close friend, ranked just after Kiera in importance.

She is committed to making decisions that benefit both herself and her friends.

Importantly, Tori understands her own boundaries, and it's essential for you to be open and accepting of the decisions she makes.

"Tore, I love you deeply. You know I trust you with my entire heart. You've truly excelled in your role as my head bartender, consistently elevating our establishment with your creativity and skill. As you know, Hailey and Dorian are moving back to Chicago tomorrow, which leaves a significant gap in our team. I'm curious about how you're feeling about Connor stepping into this territory. I realize your relationship with him is still quite new, but I can't help but think this is a fantastic opportunity for both of you to grow."

She shifts nervously in her seat, her fingers fidgeting with a loose thread on her shirt.

"I know he absolutely deserves this promotion, and it's crucial for him to lessen his worries about our situation. But honestly, it also makes me feel somewhat useless. So many of the people I care about are key figures within the Bratva, and here I am, just managing Kastaways. What's my role in all of this? Should I just settle for running a bar and never aspire to anything beyond that? Maybe I should explore a new hobby or find something that brings me fulfillment outside of this life. I'll figure it out, I promise! I just didn't mean to burden you with all of this, Kass."

I reach across the table, gently placing my hand over hers, feeling the warmth and comfort of our connection.

It's time to unveil the true purpose behind our girl time.

"Tore, you are doing just fine! I asked you for an honest answer, and that's what you've given me.

Now, let me ask you this: How do you truly feel about the Bratva brotherhood and sisterhood?"

Her eyes sparkle with enthusiasm as she meets my gaze.

"I absolutely adore the bond and fierce protectiveness that it embodies. The men, though formidable, truly care for their women, always standing as guardians, never willing to harm another woman or a child. And the sisterhood, while small, is incredibly powerful. Each of you has a unique purpose, complemented by extraordinary strength and unwavering courage. Your mission to uplift and support other women resonates deeply with me, and I can't express how much I've benefited from it. If ever given the opportunity, I would love to repay you by joining your ranks. I yearn to discover my own purpose and lend a hand to anyone in need."

Wow, that brought tears to my eyes.

"Well then, here's why I wanted to spend so much time with you today, Tori. Do you really want to join us? If you do, I have a place for you, and it's very permanent."

Her head snaps up, her expression transforming from curiosity to eagerness. "Yes! Anything! Even if it's just temporary, I want to help."

"Are you prepared to get a tattoo like Connor and Spence did? I promise ours will be smaller and cuter, something meaningful."

"Of course, Kass! Absolutely anything!"

"Do you want to know what you'll be doing permanently?" I ask, a teasing smile playing on my lips.

She smirks playfully, "Yes, my Queen!"

"You cheeky little thing! Don't call me that; it's just Kass to you! If you want it, Kastaways is yours."

Her eyes widen in disbelief. "What do you mean, Kastaways is mine?"

Just then, the waitress brought over our plates of beautifully arranged sushi, the vibrant colors of the rolls contrasting against the simple dark wood of the table.

I took a moment to dive into the deliciousness, stuffing my face and deliberately dragging out the suspense as I enjoyed the flavors.

I managed to eat six pieces before the weight of the silence became too much for her.

"Kass!!! Please explain!" she exclaimed, her voice a mix of excitement and disbelief.

I took a casual sip of my soda before responding, hiding my smile behind the glass.

"If you really want to join us, then I am signing Kastaways over to you right now. Everything about it will be in your control; you will be the sole owner. And don't worry—you'll be protected because it's in Connor's territory."

With a small, deliberate motion, I slid the neatly organized paperwork across the counter toward her, the crisp sound of the pages signaling the gravity of the moment.

Tori sat in stunned silence; her gaze fixed on the paperwork as if it held the key to a world she had always dreamt of.

"I know this is a lot, Tore, but you are ready. If you say yes, I'll take you to the tattoo parlor as soon as we leave here. And you don't have to tell anyone that you're the new owner until I'm back in two weeks for the grand reopening!"

Tears, glistening with a mixture of joy and disbelief, streamed down her cheeks as she processed the enormity of the opportunity before her.

"Yes, Kass! Thank you! You always know how to make me feel important. I won't let you down! And, of course, I'm all in for the tattoo and keeping it a secret until the grand reopening. Now you are stuck with me forever, my Queen!"

Her enthusiasm was infectious, and I couldn't help but smile brightly in response.

I wouldn't have it any other way.

Kastaways will thrive, and so will Tori.

Chapter 33

Tori

Two weeks later…

Amidst the whirlwind of preparations for the grand reopening, I find myself in a flurry of frenetic activity, all while concealing my secret identity as the new owner.

I've immersed myself in an array of marketing initiatives, pouring my energy into crafting an inviting atmosphere.

To add a touch of elegance, I had hundreds of exquisite black coasters produced, each adorned with our striking golden Kastaways logo, creating a sense of anticipation and excitement.

To further disguise my identity, I've been careful to hide my heart and tiara tattoo beneath a broad black watch band, an accessory that stands in stark contrast to the whimsical ink on my skin.

Recently, I switched my watch from my right wrist to my left, an innocent enough gesture that has not gone unnoticed.

Connor and Spencer have started to grow suspicious, their inquisitive glances hinting that my attempts at subterfuge may not be as foolproof as I had hoped, especially since I've yet to reveal why I moved the watch.

After a nerve-racking conversation between Spencer, Connor, and me, we've come to a tentative decision to explore the possibility of a romantic relationship among the three of us. It feels both exciting and a bit daunting to navigate this new dynamic.

Each night, we've been ending our evenings with silly, cheesy games that allow us to relax and laugh together.

These playful moments have become a cherished time for us to bond and peel back layers of our personalities.

From guessing each other's favorite movies to engaging in light-hearted competitions, these games have not only broken the ice but have also helped us grow closer.

Connor has been remarkably open and clear about his feelings, expressing that he's comfortable with whatever direction we choose to take.

I must admit, I was surprised by his willingness to share me.

It's a unique situation, and his laid-back attitude provides a sense of reassurance as we navigate these uncharted waters together.

However, we haven't yet crossed into full intimacy.

While we've made it to third base, we're taking our time, ensuring that we're all on the same page emotionally and physically before progressing further.

Each step we take feels significant, and I'm hopeful that this journey will bring us closer together.

Kass just texted me that she'll be arriving in one hour, marking a pivotal moment in my life—when everything becomes official.

Soon, I will officially take ownership of Kastaways, a bustling bar at the heart of the city, and in doing so, I will finally unlock my true purpose within the Bratva.

I've found myself with two loyal allies, men I trust implicitly, who stand ready to support me through this new chapter.

With Kass's arrival, I'm poised to reveal my closely guarded secret—an intricate plan that could change our future.

This is my moment to seize the opportunity that has been laid before me, and I'm ready to embrace the risks that come with it.

Chapter 34

Over the last two weeks, Tori has been running around like a whirlwind, juggling countless tasks for the highly anticipated grand reopening of Kastaways, the vibrant bar and grill with a loyal clientele.

With plates of delicious appetizers to finalize and signature cocktails to perfect, her dedication has truly been remarkable.

Kass, the original owner who launched Kastaways as her first big business venture, is flying in from out of town to celebrate this momentous occasion.

Her return is generating excitement, as she's eager to see how the place has transformed while still retaining its charm.

In the wake of Dorian and Hailey's recent move, there's been much speculation about who will be stepping in to manage operations.

Will it be someone new or perhaps a familiar face from the past?

The anticipation is palpable, and many are curious to see if the new arrivals will mesh seamlessly with Tori and the other bartenders, each of whom brings their own unique flair and personality to the team.

Kastaways is decked out in stunning gold and silver decorations that shimmer under the warm lights, creating a festive atmosphere for what is promised to be an unforgettable night.

With the bar fully stocked and the music set to energize, everything is in place for an evening to remember.

Tori has hinted at wanting to play with Connor and me tonight, so no matter what happens tonight, we will end on a high note.

Whatever happens tonight is sure to be full of excitement and new beginnings.

Chapter 35

Spencer

Kastaways is buzzing with excitement for its grand reopening, the atmosphere electric with energy as familiar faces blend with new ones.

As I scan the crowd, I see everyone who has been part of this club since my arrival—and many more who have come to celebrate this important night.

I find myself immersed in the unfolding drama and intricate politics that have come to define the very heart of Kastaways.

As a member of the Bratva, it is not only my responsibility but also my duty to gather intel and maintain a strong line of defense in this territory, ensuring its safety amidst the ever-shifting alliances.

Now, with Connor taking the reins of this domain, the stakes are higher than ever.

But beyond the club's dynamics, there is one particular presence that commands my focus: a stunning Goddess who has captured our attention and admiration, her beauty radiant even in the dim lighting of the club.

Though Tori may not be an official member of the Bratva, Connor and I share an unspoken vow to safeguard her at all costs.

Our commitment runs deep, and we would lay down our lives to protect her from the unseen dangers that lurk in the shadows of our world.

Tore is a vibrant whirlwind of energy tonight, and if I think back on the past two weeks, it's clear she's been radiating this infectious joy for quite some time.

It's as if her mind is filled with an abundance of happiness, almost clouding her thoughts in an exhilarating way.

She's nowhere close to being sad or downcast; instead, she is driven by an unwavering motivation to tackle every task thrown her way.

I can only hope that whoever steps into the leadership role at Kastaways recognizes her immense value and nurtures her ability to flourish.

According to all the staff, Kastaways would feel incomplete without her irreplaceable spirit.

My emotions for her are soaring higher than ever; I find myself at her and Connor's place every night, immersing myself in moments that bring us closer together.

We're dedicating ourselves to fortifying our bond, but it's not just my feelings for Tore that are elevating.

As I cast a glance across the room, my heart skips a beat at the sight of the striking man in the violet suit he donned months ago when he reunited with Tore.

This evening, however, he has chosen a black shirt adorned with intricate silver glittery flowers—an elegant choice that subtly echoes the attire of both Tore and myself.

My own suit, a shimmering silver, is complemented by a matching shirt that boasts its own delicate glittery floral adornments, but it's undeniably Tore who shines brightest in our ensemble.

She is wearing a breathtaking floor-length black gown, sparkling with glitter, that elegantly accentuates her every curve.

Kass, in her creativity, thought a masquerade theme was fitting once again, and Tore finds humor in its irony.

Fully recovered and embracing life, she refuses to let anything diminish her exuberant happiness.

Tonight could mark a significant turning point for the three of us, filled with deep intimacy and connection.

The Goddess has hinted that there will be ample opportunity for us to explore our desires and play together in ways that we've only begun to imagine.

It seems she has a plan in mind, something delightful and perhaps unexpectedly adventurous, which she knows we will eagerly embrace.

I find myself hoping that Connor fully immerses himself in our arrangement. I understand he is still grappling with his feelings—trying to determine whether he can support a relationship with me while simultaneously allowing me to be free with Tore.

I wish for him to reach a decision soon, but I also recognize that he needs time to navigate his emotions.

I will not pressure him into a choice, as I value our companionship at this moment.

His presence brings me comfort and joy, but deep down, my heart yearns to love and intertwine with both him and Tore.

Ultimately, I trust in the journey that lies ahead, eager to see where life takes us and what opportunities unfold in our shared path.

Chapter 36

Kass

Kastaways looks absolutely breathtaking!

The warm golden hues of the sunset reflect off the water, casting a magical glow over the venue.

I know Tori has poured her heart and soul into this place, working tirelessly to ensure that every detail is flawless and every corner exudes her unique vision.

I catch a glimpse of her behind the polished wooden bar, her true sanctuary.

It's where she thrives, surrounded by glimmering glassware and vibrant concoctions, and I genuinely hope that this remains a source of joy for her.

As Tori meets my gaze, I nod and mouth, "Are you ready?"

A spark of excitement lights up her eyes as she smiles and responds with a confident nod, "Always."

I feel a calming thrill wash over me—this is the moment we've been waiting for.

Here we go!

Kastaways will officially be Tori's!

I stride toward the stage, my heart racing as the murmurs begin to circulate through the crowd.

The anticipation is electric, and I can sense the curiosity and skepticism in the air.

Grabbing the microphone, I catch another glance at Tori.

I can tell she's picking up on the whispers as well, her determination unwavering.

With a playful twirl of her finger in the air—a signal for me that these naysayers are in for an unexpected surprise—she radiates confidence.

I adore her; she truly understands the unspoken bond we share, knowing exactly what I'm feeling in this moment of tension.

Clearing my throat, I tap gently on the microphone to draw the audience's attention, the sound echoing in the hushed space, ready to mark the beginning of an unforgettable chapter.

"As all of you know, we have made some changes to Kastaways. The first change is if you are a member of the brotherhood or sisterhood, you no longer pay a membership fee. The second change is no drama or politics is allowed in the doors of Kataways. If it is brought in, you can be banned or worse, depending on the severity. Third, you know that I am handing over Kastaway tonight."

I let them stew in that moment, their whispers intensifying and swirls of gossip weaving around the room like so many tendrils of smoke.

The air crackles with anticipation and tension, each second stretching out into what feels like an eternity.

Tori, standing behind the polished bar with her arms crossed, wears a mischievous smirk that dances across her lips.

The dim light glints off the glass in her hand, revealing the vibrant, deep crimson of the Heart of Chance, a cocktail notorious for its bittersweet flavor and intoxicating allure.

She raises her glass to me in a playful toast, her eyes sparkling with delight as she relishes the chaos unfolding just as much as I do.

It's a shared moment of exhilaration, a deliciously wicked thrill that pulses through the atmosphere, binding us in this delightful game of uncertainty and intrigue.

I tap the microphone and continue, "Just because someone else is taking over does not mean I will not show up. In my hand, I have the necklace of the individual taking over Kastaways. Anyone of our women who wears a necklace such as this in the shape of a heart is not to be messed with. If they are, there will be dire consequences! This exquisite heart necklace, glimmering with brilliance, is a cherished gift for a radiant star—an unwavering pillar within Kastaways. Their presence is a source of strength and inspiration, deeply valued not just by me but by countless others in our community. Their spirit shines so brightly that nothing can ever dull their brilliance. This stunning violet heart will grace their neck for all time, a symbol of love and appreciation that will forever capture their unique sparkle."

I take a moment to let the tension in the room settle, allowing everyone to arrive at their own conclusions.

Tori, her eyes narrowing with determination, put her drink down and readied herself for what was about to unfold.

The murmurs around the table grow louder, underscoring the unease in the air; people are getting ridiculous in their speculations.

"Who is this outsider coming to take over our club?" one voice whispers incredulously, a hint of disbelief lacing their tone.

"Why would the Queen so easily relinquish control?" another adds, their brow furrowed in confusion.

"Nobody can run this place like Dorian!" a third interjects, the nostalgia evident in their voice as they reminisce about the old days of Dorian's leadership.

I can't help but smirk at their anxious reactions.

"Remember, everyone, this newcomer has the authority to terminate any membership at any time! This person now holds more power than I ever did within these walls. They call the shots here." I turn to face the group fully, my demeanor shifting to one of seriousness. "Violet, Kastaways is officially yours."

As I say her name, I can feel the weight of the room shift. The whispers hush, leaving a palpable anticipation hanging in the air, its gravity sinking in as everyone realizes the implications of the moment.

The Violet Reign begins.

Chapter 37

G.W.

You have got to be fucking kidding me?

Tori, of all people!

I've finally figured it out!

What we had was purely casual, but maybe I can persuade her to give me a job as a bartender at the club.

That way, I'll have the perfect opportunity to get close to her and tap into the fortune she's recently acquired.

There are whispers circulating that she's involved with not one but two members of the Bratva.

It's a dangerous game, but the allure of her connection to their world is tempting.

To be honest, I struggled even to sleep with her due to her size; the thought of a woman over 200 pounds isn't something that typically appeals to me.

For me, our encounters were just a way to satisfy a fleeting desire.

Yet, the idea of rekindling that physical connection is becoming increasingly enticing, especially if it means gaining access to the wealth that seems to flow through her life now.

Let's face it: the world doesn't need more curvy women; it craves the glamour and allure of models.

The world doesn't need women in authoritative positions; women belong in the bead and the kitchen, that's it.

Chapter 38

Tore!!!

She owns Kastaways now? That's a huge step!

Why didn't she share this news with me or anyone else in the circle?

She's wearing the Bratva tattoo and the necklace now—what's the fuck?

What prompted this sudden change in her life?

Did Kass encourage her decision, or was there some pressure involved?

By taking on this role, she's reached the same level as me in the Bratva—does she fully grasp the responsibilities that come with it?

What made her shift her perspective so dramatically?

Will she still make time for me amidst all these new commitments?

Will she still prioritize our relationship, or will the demands of her new position come first?

What about Spence?

I guess she really is the Goddess of the Bratva now, living up to the title in every way.

Chapter 39

Spencer

My Goddess!

She radiates brilliance!

With her guidance, Kastaways will ascend to a realm of excellence and prosperity!

No one will dare to lay a finger on her; we will be her unwavering shield.

I can't help but wonder what thoughts swirl through Connor's mind.

Well, it looks like I am about to find out.

Connor is tromping over here.

His face flushed, tight fists, and heavy breathing.

"Did you know? Spence, don't lie to me!"

Does he think I was behind this?

"Calm down, CC. I was just as shocked as you are. But there has to be an explanation; I am sure she will tell us all about it. We should be extremely excited for her and be there to support and encourage her. She has decided to take this step and join us; let's hear her out when we get the chance and tell her how proud of her we are."

He lets out a soft sigh, his shoulders gently easing as he speaks, "But what about us, Spence? Will she have the time to nurture our bond, or will we fade into the background? She knows how deeply I adore her, but does she realize that our love for her transcends mere affection? Does she understand that she is our divine muse, the center of our universe? That she is the very breath in my lungs? In our eyes, can she do no wrong, and can her every flaw be transformed into a unique beauty? That nothing in this world could ever come close to the depth of our love for her?"

Does he realize that is the first time he has acknowledged that the three of us are a couple?

I put my hand on his shoulder and caressed his arm, "Chance, you just admitted that the three of us are a couple. You know you have never said it out loud until you did just now. Do you realize my feelings are growing for you as much as my feelings are growing for Tori? I always knew I was bisexual, but it took the sexiest guy to bring me to life. We will get through this together, the three of us. Maybe we can talk before we play tonight."

We were so entranced that we didn't hear our Goddess walks up.

"How about we go talk now? Because I need to play with you both."

Connor and my gazes snap to the blonde beauty, all it takes is a nod and we are on our way.

Chapter 40

Okay, the plan just got dangerous.

She is talking to the commander and the attorney.

Are they the two she's sleeping with?

What do they see in her?

Where is she taking them?

Are they going to play tonight?

Is she truly that reckless in her romantic relationships, or does she get off on the danger?

Or perhaps she is simply using them to her advantage?

They possess an immense amount of wealth and influence—far beyond anything she could ever hope to attain on her own.

That's the conclusion I've reached: she's nothing more than a gold digger, strategically leveraging their resources to elevate her own status and lifestyle.

Kass can only get her so far.

But I will bring her to her knees; she will fall at my feet!

Game on, Violet!

Your skin will be violet before I am done with you!

Chapter 41

Tori

I guide my comrades to the library, relishing the tranquility it offers—its soundproof walls create an atmosphere of hushed reverence, broken only by the occasional shuffle of pages unless you venture upstairs to the viewing room.

This elusive space, accessible solely from the first floor, requires a subtle request to the bartender, who will grant passage only to those adorned with a shimmering gold bracelet.

The exclusive nature of the viewing room adds an air of mystery, inviting curiosity about the secrets it holds within.

"Sit! You both will listen to meand then I'll decide if we'll play, okay?"

They slowly turn to face each other, their expressions a mix of anticipation and submission.

Connor confidently rests his hand on Spence's knee, a gentle yet deliberate gesture that speaks volumes about their dynamic.

Tell me, why does that moment feel so intoxicatingly sexy?

In unison, they respond, "Yes, Goddess," their voices laced with eagerness and devotion, sending a thrill through me.

I had to catch my breath; that simple exchange made my knees weak with desire.
Obedience does it for me—there's something undeniably alluring about it, yes, please!

"I am laying it all out for you both, fully and honestly. Nobody knew that I was taking over tonight except for me, Kass, and Massimo. Kass, being resourceful as always, used your partner, Spence, to help keep this under wraps, swearing him to secrecy to avoid any misunderstandings. I finalized and signed the contract two weeks ago—an act that felt monumental—and I even went as far as getting the tattoo to symbolize my commitment and readiness for this new chapter. I had a reason behind this decision. Both of you hold significant roles within the Bratva, and I realized I needed a purpose of my own. You have both dedicated so much time and effort to ensuring I recover properly, nurturing my growth and healing, and I didn't want to feel like a burden or be left feeling useless anymore. When Kass presented me with the opportunity, she made it clear that while she wanted me to take on this responsibility, she also cared for my well-being. She offered me a choice between managing Kastaways or taking full ownership. After careful consideration, I chose ownership. I wanted to stand firmly for what the Bratva represents—strength, loyalty, and community—and I felt a calling to contribute in a meaningful way. This decision was entirely mine, driven by the desire to prove myself and to give back. Just as loving you both is my choice, this path I've chosen reflects my commitment to us and the Bratva as a whole."

Spence glances over at Connor, his expression softening with understanding.

He gently takes his hand off Connor's knee and intertwines his fingers with his, their palms warm and reassuring against each other.

I can't help but observe that as their hands connect, Connor visibly relaxes, the tension in his shoulders easing.

It becomes clear to me that this moment holds weight for him; he must have been facing something challenging, and Spence's gesture offers him a sense of comfort and support that he desperately needs.

Connor lets out a deep, heavy sigh, his brow furrowing with concern.

"I feared, truly feared, that you wouldn't love us as we love you. I worried you would be consumed by everything else, leaving us feeling like an afterthought. But now I see it's us who have put you second when you should always be our undisputed first. You are our goddess, capable of incredible things, and in our eyes, you can do no wrong. I recognize that this journey is still fresh for all of us, but, as Spence wisely said, we will navigate these uncharted waters together. I want you to know how deeply I love you—but it's equally important to let us love you back. Allow us to stand resolutely by your side, helping you embrace your reign. Kastaways is your domain now; your word is law, and no one can challenge that. We are here, unwavering, every step of the way, ensuring you have everything you need, and no one can take this from you. We've witnessed the strength you've unearthed through your recovery, and, yes, perhaps we've spoiled you a bit too much. Yet we take immense pride in the progress you've made; you've emerged from that shadowy place, and we are so proud of you. Whatever choices you make, we will always be here. I lost my chance with you once, and I won't allow that to happen again. Spence is precisely the balm I needed; he keeps me grounded, revealing parts of myself I never knew existed. His love and affection for you only draw me closer to him, weaving us together in an unexpected tapestry of connection. Never in a million years did I envision being part of a throuple, but here we are, and I couldn't be happier. So let's claim this territory together, not just with fierce determination, but with boundless love and care."

Spence gently cupped his face in his hands and pressed a soft kiss to his cheek; the affection between those two warms my heart.

 "There's not much I can add to what's been said, Goddess, but I want you to know that we'll be here for every moment of this journey, good and bad. I can feel the love growing stronger between all of us with each passing day. It's a bond that no one can take away from us. You and Connor have truly brought out the best in me, and I believe together, we can run this territory with you firmly at the helm. With your leadership, I have no doubt that no one would dare to cross us. Also, I've been thinking about taking a step that might solidify our unity even further—how would you both feel if I moved down here permanently? Massimo has already given his approval for the transfer, but I didn't want to overstep any boundaries or make you feel pressured. Your feelings mean the world to me, and I want to ensure that this decision aligns with what's best for all of us."

He really puts his heart on his sleeve.

I step forward and simultaneously caress their cheeks.

"I have no doubts about us; this throuple means everything and more to me. The bond we share is a unique tapestry woven with trust, love, and shared experiences, and I cherish it deeply. The experience of owning Kastaways fills me with a profound sense of purpose and offers a fulfilling distraction while you both pursue your individual passions and dreams. I promise to establish firm boundaries in my professional life, ensuring that my work remains separate from our cherished relationship so that it will never overshadow the love and intimacy we share. I envision us spreading love throughout the community here, just like Kass does so beautifully in Chicago. Kastaways should not be seen merely as an elite social club but rather as a welcoming, safe haven for those who need it, a place where everyone feels accepted and valued. Life can be incredibly challenging, and it is vital for people to have a nurturing space where they can find solace and support. Together, let's cultivate an atmosphere that fosters kindness and connection, ensuring that no one feels alone in their struggles."

"Spoken like a true Goddess."

I smile, "Are we ready to play? We are in the library, and I just educated you, so it's only fitting that we have some fun."

The lust on their faces says it all; this could be quite the adventure.

Chapter 42

G.W.

She leads them to the library, but why?

That is not a very kinky room; maybe the rumors are false.

I make my way to the top floor, my golden bracelet on display; I need to know what they are talking about.

I reach the first floor bartender and ask to be let in to the viewing room of the library, she checks my bracelet then leads the way.

She motions to the box in the room; it's the soundbox.

I turn it on so I can hear what they are saying.

"Are we ready to play? We are in the library, and I just educated you, so it's only fitting that we have some fun."

Shit!

It seems I missed their entire conversation, but that's alright; I'm sure I'll uncover the details soon enough.

From what I've observed, Connor and Spencer exhibit an unusual level of obedience whenever Tori is present.

I can't help but wonder what lies behind that behavior.

In my interactions with Tori, she hasn't come across as particularly authoritative—she lacks the commanding presence one might expect.

Connor stood tall, a fierce determination etched across his face. "If the Goddess wishes it, let it be so!" he proclaimed, his voice resonating with conviction.

Goddess?

Was that really her nickname?

It sounded almost ridiculous.

Surely, no one could genuinely want to worship someone with a figure like hers.

It felt like a cruel joke, a mocking title that didn't truly reflect her reality.

How could anyone revere a mere mortal in a way reserved for divine beings?

The only thing divine about her is her bank account!

"I wish that both of you would bow at my feet, naked."

Okay, so maybe she has finally found her confidence now.

That is a stark contrast to our past experiences, where it often felt like we were merely fulfilling a singular purpose.

Tori appears to have a clear vision of what she desires, but one has to wonder—will she really be able to balance the attention of both men at once?

It's quite striking to witness men of such stature and influence respond so instantly to her commands; seeing powerful men display such obedience creates an unsettling atmosphere.

If I were in their position, I would make sure she followed every word I said without question.

They didn't question her; they just took off their clothes and sat at her feet!

A flush of embarrassment washes over her.

With a subtle but determined movement, she reaches beside her and begins to unzip her dress. The soft sound of the zipper gliding down fills the air, creating a sense of anticipation.

As she peels the fabric away, the dress slips gracefully over her head, cascading down her body until she's left standing in her delicate thong.

How can the men at her feet be salivating?

They look like they are ready to make a full meal out of her; she isn't even a satisfying snack.

The way their eyes roam over her body is appalling; no one wants to see that.

"Can we touch you, Goddess?"

Did the Commander of this territory just ask a mere woman for permission?

I have lost respect for Connor, and I refuse to follow a woman's directions.

Following those directions and asking for permission is what makes men look weak.

"Touch me, love me! Do your worst!"

Tori's whole body is flushing as both men caress her.

Connor is in front of her, still on his knees; he is stroking her inner thighs.

Spencer has moved behind her; he is trailing kisses down her back, looks like he's a licker.

Gross!

Who would want to lick a body that big?

"I want to be dirty! Use me! Get your fill!"

Why is Tori so into this?

What is it about these men that captivates Tori?

What qualities do they possess that I lack?

I stand at six foot five, with a physique sculpted from years of disciplined training and a history marked by military service.

My gray hair, a distinguishing feature, speaks not of age but of the countless hardships I have endured—particularly in the realm of relationships.

Having faced the pain of divorce, I know the bitter taste of betrayal all too well.

My ex-wife attempted to seize what little savings I managed to hold on to after our separation, leaving me wary and distrustful.

It's precisely these experiences that have shaped my approach toward women; I find myself targeting those who, I believe, share the same capacity for deception that I have encountered.

In my mind, they deserve to feel the weight of their wrongdoings—as I have.

My resolve is firm: as long as my carefully laid plan unfolds without a hitch, I will reclaim the financial losses that have haunted me for years.

Tori, with her seemingly effortless charm and the affluence that comes so easily to her, is emblematic of everything I resent.

She does not deserve the wealth that life has bestowed upon her, not when I am still picking up the pieces of my own shattered dreams.

These men are worshipping her; she doesn't deserve that.

She deserved to be choked and suffocated; she didn't belong in this world.

No one would miss her if she disappeared!

"Goddess, I need to feel you! Where can I go? Tell me what you want! Tell me what you need!"

Shut up, Connor. No one wants to hear you whine; you, the Commander, act like it!

"I need you both to fill me! Don't hold back! Bend me! Break me!"

She's begging!

She never begged me, what the hell?

Spencer, a toned older gentleman with gray hair, yanks Tori's head back.

"You want us to fill you? Do you want it rough, Goddess?"

Spencer licks Tori's ear, and she shivers," Yes! Rough! I won't break!"

This is what she likes?

I could give her this; we never played here.

Our sex was generic, but if I knew she was into things like this, we could've made sparks fly.

Spencer takes charge, "Front or back, Chance?"

Connor glances at Spencer.

It seems there is some kind of connection there, but I can't place it.

Connor leans over Tori to reach Spencer; he grabs his head and thrusts his face against his.

That's the first time I have seen two men kiss; I am conflicted.
Their kiss made my heart flutter; that was hot.

"I want the front so that I can see the Goddess and the Prince climax. Don't hold back; I love it when you are loud. Are you ready for us, Goddess? I can feel how soaked you are."

Connor continues to play with Tori's pussy; her moans keep getting louder.

"Fuck me! I am so fucking ready!"

Connor just glances at Spencer again, and Tori notices this time.

"Way to keep me in the dark, guys! What are we doing? You can't just play with me all night!"

Connor and Spencer chuckled at each other.

Connor moans in Tori's ear, "Goddess, the dark can't handle what we have in store for you!"

At that moment, Spencer spits in his hand and rubs into Tori's ass crack.

Umm, what is he doing?

"Oh shit!"

Spencer enters her from behind as Connor kisses her lips.

Again, I don't know how to feel right now; I have never watched anyone be this intimate.

I feel the blood rushing to my dick.

Connor tears his lips from Tori's and thrusts into her vagina.

"Yes! Don't stop! Harder! Chance! Spence!"

Holy shit!

Tori is about to climax; I might have to rub one out.

As I adjust myself, Connor claps, and the library goes dark.

"Yes! Yes! Now! More! Fuuuuccck!"

What happened?

Why did the lights go out?

Why couldn't I see her finish?

Fuck!

Now I am going to be thinking about that all night!

Maybe my new kink is voyeurism.

Let me get out of here before someone realizes I have been her.

Tonight has been a ride.

A ride I will be enjoying again.

Chapter 43

Tori

One week later…

This week has been nothing short of a whirlwind of passion and discovery!

Every couple of days, I find myself immersed in the most exhilarating sexual experiences of my life.

Who would have thought that it would take not one but two captivating men to awaken this side of me?

Connor has always held a special place in my heart, but now my feelings have deepened, and I can't bear the thought of losing him.

He has transformed immensely as an individual, and the way he looks at me makes me feel as if the entire universe is resting in my hands.

He inspires me to embrace my potential and reminds me that failure is simply not an option.

Connor's impressive height and sculpted physique are certainly appealing, yet what truly captivates me is the essence of the vibrant young boy I fell in love with.

Now, I am gradually witnessing the emergence of a strong, stoic man who is rediscovering his own radiance.

Then there's Spence, a delightful surprise in my life.

Who knew that a girl like me could attract a powerful, charismatic man in his late forties?

While he may be beyond the typical age of desirability, his youthful vigor defies expectations.

When I see Connor and Spence together, it feels like I'm gazing at the epitome of Greek sculptures — their bodies are chiseled, their jawlines sharply defined, and their broad shoulders exude strength and confidence.

Add to that luscious hair — Connor boasts rich brown locks while Spence wears his distinguished gray with an allure that is hard to resist. It's amusing to think that women often pay a fortune for the very gray hair that men possess naturally.

I say let them keep it because there's something undeniably attractive about it!

Kastaways has been thriving beyond our wildest expectations; every night, the bar is packed to the brim with lively patrons enjoying their favorite drinks and good company.

I have stayed true to my commitment to my team; I've learned to leave work behind when I step out of these doors, allowing myself to truly unwind.

Shannon, our new head bartender, has been busy scouting for a fresh face to join our team, and it seems she's found a promising candidate I'll be meeting with shortly.

It's crucial that we find someone who can seamlessly blend with the lively vibe we've cultivated here.

We need someone fun—someone who knows how to keep the energy high.

Someone outgoing who can engage customers with ease and charm.

Someone who's willing to let loose and join in the revelry when it calls for it.

Someone who possesses the finesse to maintain control over the crowd, ensuring everyone has a fantastic time while also keeping an eye on things.

Someone with a huge, infectious smile that lights up the room—someone who can brighten even the gloomiest of days.

Ideally, this person won't require extensive training; we need someone who can jump right in and start contributing from day one.

They should fit in effortlessly, forging strong connections with both the staff and our diverse clientele.

As I sift through the paperwork that has accumulated on my desk throughout the day, I suddenly feel a familiar presence approaching me.

"Miss me, sugar?"

Ugh…

What on earth is he doing here?

Goodness, I absolutely detest that nickname!

"Can I help you, Gabe? I have a very important interview that I am waiting for! So, if you will excuse me, I don't have time to scratch your itch."

He chuckles, "I am your interview, sugar."

"Are you really pulling my leg right now? Are you telling me you're the interviewee Shannon set up for me? What kind of bartending experience do you even have? It's been months since you last called or texted, and now you walk in here unexpectedly as my interview candidate. I have to say, I'm not comfortable with this situation at all. You'll need to do a lot of convincing if you want me to consider hiring you. We have a complicated history that doesn't belong in the workplace. If I were to bring you on board, can you guarantee that you'll keep things professional, or do you think that might pose a problem?"

He smirks at me; he knows what that smirk does to me.

"Sugar, I do anything you tell me to. But why are you interviewing me? I thought the owner was interviewing me?"

This dumbass.

"No way, you don't get to play dumb, Gabriel! I saw you; you were at the grand reopening! What do you want? I do not have time for games."

"I'm eager to find a job, Sugar. I'd love to help you out at the bar. With extensive bartending training and a wealth of experience working in various clubs along the coast, I believe I could be a valuable asset. I'm here nearly every night, so I'm quite familiar with your menu and can craft just about any drink on it. However, I'm still trying to master the Heart of Chance. It's one of your signature creations, and while I find it absolutely delightful, I haven't yet cracked the recipe. I've been experimenting to recreate that unique flavor at home, but there's something about your version that makes it truly special."

I think, "Duh, of course, there's something special about it. First, it's my signature drink, crafted during a particularly challenging chapter of my life that you probably know nothing about, given your reluctance to engage in meaningful conversations. Secondly, you wouldn't be able to recreate it even if you tried since you don't have my secret recipe, and let me be clear: you won't be making Heart of Chance here, even if you get the job. The only two people permitted to mix that drink are Shannon and me. You must understand one crucial thing, Gabriel: this is my club. What I say goes, and I won't tolerate any disrespect directed at Shannon, me, my creations, or my establishment. Let's be honest: I'm not even certain I want to hire you. It's been almost five months since you last reached out, and I must ask: do you truly believe you deserve a chance to be part of my legacy? Yes, I said my legacy. Kass saw potential in me, and I refused to let her down. This is my club, and I'm determined to see it thrive! If you want to be part of that vision, you're going to have to beg for it—especially since you chose to disappear for months before resurfacing."

Okay, that was very bitchy of me.

Do I regret it?

Nope, not a bit.

He doesn't know what I have gone through and has not even checked on me, so he deserves the hostility.

"Sugar, you want me to beg? Is that what you're into?"

His voice is low, teasing, laced with a hint of challenge as he locks eyes with me.

Without waiting for a response, he drops to his knees, the cool floor pressing against him as he grips my leg with a gentle yet firm hold.

The sudden shift in power dynamics sends a jolt of electricity through me.

Why is my heart racing like this? Every thump feels like it's echoing in the silence between us.

There's something intoxicating about seeing Gabe on his knees, looking up at me with that playful glint in his eyes. It stirs a mixture of excitement and vulnerability that I can't quite put into words.

"Sugar, I believe in this opportunity! Hire me, and I will wholeheartedly commit to following your and Shannon's guidance. I'll keep things professional unless you want me to explore a different dynamic. My dedication to you and the club is unwavering. Let me show you what I can do!"

That was so satisfying and sexy.

Stay professional, Tore!

I roll my eyes, "Fine! You have one chance! I am so pissed at you, so don't fuck this up!"

Chapter 44

Gabriel Wright

It unfolded even better than I had anticipated, each moment twisting perfectly into place like pieces of a well-crafted puzzle.

She remains utterly malleable in my grasp, her vulnerabilities laid bare beneath my calculated charm.

Unbeknownst to her, I have a series of carefully orchestrated plans in motion, intricately designed to draw her in, one charming smile at a time.

The prospect of indulging in another fleeting moment with her is enticing, igniting a thrill that races through me with each passing day.

Yet, it's a perilous game I've chosen to play—one that requires constant vigilance around two formidable men, her steadfast guardians, who seem ever-watchful.

Or should I refer to them as her ever-vigilant sentinels? Their loyalty to her is commendable, but it also stirs a deep-seated irritation within me.

It never ceases to astound me how dutifully they obey her every command; their eagerness to serve her wishes is utterly distasteful, a bitter pill I must swallow for now.

I will don my mask of compliance and play my part flawlessly until I secure the desires I crave most.

I'll layer on the charm, employing every tactic at my disposal, to see just how long Tori can withstand my alluring presence.

Shannon has provided me with the vital details necessary for when the game finally commences, knowing the key moments that will shift the tides in my favor.

Before I dive into my strategy next week, I have a few tricks waiting in the wings, each meticulously planned to heighten the tension.

First, I'll swing by the barbershop for a crisp, fresh cut that will undoubtedly make Tori weak in the knees, sharp enough to catch her eye from across the room.

Next, a trip to the mall is absolutely non-negotiable; I need snug-fitting pants that accentuate my physique and stylish shirts that scream confidence to complete the ensemble.

The tighter the clothes, the easier it will be to manipulate these women into believing I am the man they never knew they needed.

Before long, Tori will be virtually entranced by my calculated presence, caught in the web I weave.

But fear not Sugar; I promise I'll handle your heart with delicate care, even as I play the master of this dangerous game.

Chapter 45

Connor

What the fuck did I just see?

I know my Goddess loves begging, but something is off about that man.

I am texting Spence to see what he can find about this Gabe character.

When he was begging, it looked like he knew Tori's weakness.

No one touches what is ours without our permission.

She didn't know I saw the encounter, but I am not one to hide my feelings anymore.

"Tori, what the fuck was that? Who is that, and why was he touching you like that? Do I need to kill him?"

Why the hell is she laughing at me?

"Chance, we are a throuple, and you really have the nerve to get jealous?"

I feel emotions rising, "Tore, think again. What did you just say to me?"

"You have the nerve to get jealous? I have seen the way you and Spence have been acting when I am not looking. I know about the other night when I was showering. I heard you, Connor. Y'all were fucking in my bed, am I jealous? No, that's part of the dynamic we are in; you and Spence are allowed to be intimate. You're jealous of a man touching me in a nonsexual way? Why is that?"

My blood is boiling.

I step towards her, my fingers slowly wrapping around my neck.

"I have a right to be jealous; you were mine first. I am not jealous of Spence; who is the guy that touched you? How do you know him?"

She sighs, "We had a situationship. We just had sex every now and then. We have not slept together since before my incident."

What?

"His name?"

"Oh geez, Gabriel Wright. Why?"

I loosen my grip on her neck, "Because I need to know if he is a competition or someone you want to die."

She wiggles in my grasp, her frustration palpable as she glares at me, fire sparking in her eyes. "Fuck you! I don't have to justify my past relationships to you," she snaps, her voice laced with defiance. "Are you really that curious about how we were together? Do you think he knows me better than you do?"

The tension between us thickens, and I can feel the weight of her words hanging in the air, challenging me to confront my insecurities.

I hoist her over my shoulder, "I will show you how well I know you! You will never question how well I know you. We are going to the office playroom."

Her legs tighten around me, making me want to fuck her right here and now.

"What why? You can't still be mad! Chance, come on!"

"Nice try, Goddess. Calling me by your favorite pet name will prevent you from this. I'm going to your favorite thing."

As I kick the door to the office playroom in, her legs tighten around me again.

"You don't mean what I think you mean?"

She is squirming and rubbing her cooch on my crotch.

She knows exactly what I am talking about.

"Yes, Tore. I know you remember the night I ate your pussy in your dad's office. I am going to make you squirm, squirt, and scream. I will be tasting you for days. You were mine first! So, I will show how much I know your body. I will not hold back! I am pissed and jealous, so I need this, and I need you!

We are going to record this for Spence; I triggered the camera when we walked in. You ready, Goddess?"

"Do I have a choice? I feel like this is an angry fuck."

That is exactly what this is.

I don't give her a chance to say anything else.

I throw her on the couch and lunge on top of her; this is where she belongs.

I place my head tightly around her neck as I finger her through her thong.

"You're not thinking of anyone else right now, are you, Goddess?"

Her moan tells me all I need to know.

I slide down her body.

I kiss up her thighs and flip her leather skirt up towards her belly button.

I rip her black lacy thong with my teeth; I will buy her as many as she desires.

"Mine. Spence's. No one else's until we say so!"

"You do.."

She can't even finish the sentence because my head dives between her legs.

Her scent, an intoxicating blend of lust and sweet vanilla, lingers in my memory like a vivid dream—a warm aroma that envelops the senses and draws you in.

It's the kind of fragrance that dances at the edges of my mind, evoking images of sultry summer nights and whispered promises, a reminder of moments that are both tantalizing and unforgettable.

Her fingers dig into my back; she loves this!

She is squirting all over my face as her moans fill the room.

I know her body so well; she is thirty seconds from having an orgasm.

I pick up my pace, lapping up her sweet juices.

As I feel her tensing and getting ready to climax, I quickly undo my belt and thrust into her.

Thrust.

"You."

Thrust.

"Are."

Thrust.

"OWNED."

Thrust.

"BY."

Thrust.

"US!"

Thrust.

Thrust.

"You."

Thrust.

"WILL."

Thrust.

Thrust.

"Ask."

Thrust.

"For permission."

Thrust.

Thrust.

"If you."

Thrust.

"Want."

Thrust.

Thrust.

"Anyone else."

Thrust.

"TO."

Thrust.

Thrust.

I am so fucking close, my body is on fire!

"TOUCH."

FUCK!

I can't hold it back!

Thrust.

"YOU!"

"YES, CHANCE! FUCK!"

We climax together, entangled in each other's scents, craving this moment now and forever.

I kiss her forehead, "Never doubt our love, Tore. We will move heaven and hell for you."

Chapter 46

Tori

What in the fuck was that?

That is the question that stays in my head as I am cleaning up and using the bathroom.

I have never been fucked like that!

Did I love it?

Yes!

That was the hottest thing that ever happened to me; I never imagined that I would fully be immersed in a possessive hate fuck.

I have come to truly embrace Chance's profound lesson: I cannot expect unwavering obedience from others if I fail to embody it myself.

Yes, I have returned to calling him Chance, a name that now resonates deeply with the rekindled love I feel for him.

In my life's journey, he truly represents the best chance I ever took—a risk that has beautifully transformed into an unwavering connection.

Every day, I feel my love for Spence blossoming more deeply. He is truly one of a kind, with a charisma that draws me in like no other.

What strikes me the most is how effortlessly he manages to tame Chance, balancing his exuberance with how he elegantly guides me.

Despite his firm control, I always feel cherished and empowered, never once diminished—like a Goddess in my own right.

Both Spence and Chance have unique ways of showering me with affection.

Spence has a knack for surprising me with thoughtful gestures, while Chance fills our days with laughter and spontaneity.

I genuinely wouldn't have it any other way; their love enriches my life in ways I never imagined possible.

But then there's the unexpected issue of Gabe waltzing back into my life as if he hadn't left at the worst time in my life.

What we once had felt painfully generic, nothing more than a routine of predictable conversations lacking any real spark or passion.

Yet, when I found him begging for another chance, a fire ignited within me that I hadn't anticipated.

Seeing him on his knees, vulnerability etched across his face, stirred desires in my mind that I never knew I harbored for him.

It was as if the walls I had built around my heart began to crumble, revealing a longing that both excited and terrified me.

Chapter 47

Gabriel

One week later…

Today is the day!

I'm stepping into my role as the new bartender at Kastaways, and I can already feel the thrill of anticipation coursing through me.

But there's a little twist: my new boss has been trying to reach me, and I've chosen to let her calls go straight to voicemail.

Every time her name flashes on my phone, I revel in the idea of making her confront me face-to-face.

She's been circling around me, but today, she won't escape.

I plan to make her squirm a little when we finally meet.

After all, she can't avoid me forever—especially since her authority now lies in my hands behind the bar.

I can't help but wonder what kind of mischief I might stir up today!

As I make my way to work, I can't help but think about how much fun it will be to tease her before we open up for the day.

I still remember the way she reacted when I playfully begged her for a little attention, it was like a spark ignited in her eyes, filled with desire.

I could tell that if I kept pushing, she might just forget about Connor and Spencer completely, consumed by the moment we were sharing.

There's something about her that draws me in, and I can't shake the feeling that she deserves more than what those two can offer.

Connor and Spencer have been friends for a while now, but the question lingers in my mind: are they really in a romantic relationship?

The dynamic among the three of them is complex.

As I approach the office, I wonder what the day will bring and whether I'll get the chance to make my plan fall into place.

Chapter 48

Tori

Why won't Gabe answer my calls?

I've tried reaching him multiple times, but each attempt sends me directly to voicemail, which is frustrating.

I wanted to have a serious conversation about terminating his contract; I believe it's essential to maintain clear boundaries between our personal and professional lives, especially after the way he's been acting lately.

Shannon has also been trying to get in touch with him for days, but she hasn't had any luck either.

This silence is becoming increasingly concerning, and I can't shake the feeling that something isn't right.

He needs a good-ass whooping!

Spence is supposed to be dropping by tonight; he sounded quite troubled and hinted that he needed to discuss something important.

Spence hasn't moved in with us yet; he mentioned that for the time being, he still values having his own space.

He enjoys the independence of living alone and feels it allows him to recharge after a long day.

Although he appreciates our company and the idea of sharing a home, he's not quite ready to give up the comfort of his own apartment just yet.

Connor showed Spence the video of us in the office playroom.

He also explained why he was so mad.

That same night Spence claimed my ass while Connor watched; that was his version of an angry fuck.

Spence told me that if I couldn't learn to obey him and Connor that they would fuck more often without me.

Does that make me jealous?

I'm jealous that I can't watch, but I'm never jealous that they are pursuing their feelings.

I wouldn't want any other men to love me; they make me feel like I can fly.

There's a soft knock on my office door; it sounds like it could be Spence.

"Come in, baby. I've missed you!"

Chapter 49

Gabriel

Oʜ...

She must think it's one of her men; I will play this up.

"Oh, sugar. I missed you too. The things I want to do to you!"

She spins around as I walk into the office, her face flushed red.

Her eyes go wide with recognition.

"Don't you dare talk to me that way! I am your boss! You will respect me, or you will get the fuck out of my club!"

She slams her fist on the polished wooden desk, the force sending a shudder through the scattered papers and coffee mug.

Her eyes flash with intensity, a spark of frustration mixed with determination, while the room fills with a tense silence.

It's clear that someone is feeling particularly feisty tonight, ready to unleash their pent-up energy and emotions.

"Sugar, I'm just teasing you! You sparked this playful banter by calling me 'baby.' I promise I won't do it again—cross my heart! Unless, of course, you'd like me to keep it going."

I step towards her, caress her cheek and whisper, "You know what I can do to that big ass body of yours. Let me remind you how it feels to be mine!"

Her breath is speeding up, perfect!

Come back to me, Tori!

Chapter 50

"You know what I can do to that big ass body of yours. Let me remind you how it feels to be mine!"

Over my dead body!

I kick the door in, snatch the boy by the back of his neck, and slam him against the office wall.

I rush and grab the front of his neck, gripping it like my life depends on it.

I growl at him, "Gabriel Wright, you are dumber than your father! How dare you touch someone who doesn't belong to you? How dare you disrespect your boss! If you want to live, I suggest you leave and never show your face at Kastaways again! Your membership and employment have been terminated, effective immediately! Keep your hands to yourself! Your actions can and will get you killed."

I release his neck.

He struggles to catch his breath.

"You have no idea who you're truly up against! Tori, are you really going to allow your ferocious guard dog to treat me this way? You need to assert your authority! Remember, you were mine before any of this happened! He doesn't genuinely want you; his eyes are set on your other protector! Walk away from them and reclaim what is rightfully ours!"

I raise my hand to smack him; the Goddess saves the peasant.

SMACK!

Oh shit!

Never mind, damn, that could have been heard across the street!

Tori smacked him so hard his head could've turned 360 degrees!

Shit, I kind of feel bad for him.

I hope she never hits me like that!

"You said the wrong thing, Gabe! I was Connor's first love before I ever became yours! When I needed love and support the most, you just vanished! You weren't there during my darkest moments. Who stood by my side? My guard dogs and Kass! And before you even think of dismissing this, let me remind you that Kass showed me her texts to you! Your response was a mere 'K'—so casual and cold. I wanted to believe you could change, that you could make up for your indifference, which is why I offered you that job. But now, with how you've acted, you've completely shattered that chance! Get the hell out of my life and never come back! I will never be yours again!"

"Tori ple.."

"GET THE FUCK OUT! BEFORE I KILL YOU!"

He looks at the floor, "Yes, ma'am. I am sorry, Sugar."

He walks out of the office; I watch the security cameras to ensure he leaves the building.

"He's gone, Goddess."

She sighs, "Good fucking riddance. I gave him too many chances."

"You have no idea. I'm calling Connor, but we have a lot to talk about."

Tore and Connor are going to flip when I tell them what I found out about Gabriel.

Chapter 51

Tori

I decided to put Shannon in charge for the night.

After the whole debacle with Gabe, I realized I really needed a night to unwind and recharge.

Spence promptly called his driver, and soon, we were in route to our home to meet Connor for an important conversation.

I felt the weight of the day slowly lifting, but I knew a stress reliever was exactly what I needed.

As we approached the car, Spence opened my door with the kind of gentlemanly grace that always surprised me.

I slipped inside, feeling the warmth of the leather upholstery wrap around me like a comforting embrace.

Once we were settled, he gave the driver our destination, and with a soft click, the divider was raised, isolating us from the outside world.

I could feel the tension in the air shift as he gently caressed my leg, his touch igniting a spark of longing within me.

In that moment, I was certain about what I wanted, and I was ready to show Spence how I feel.

I slide out of my seat and onto the floor of the vehicle.

I rub my palms up and down his legs.

"Goddess, what are you doing? It's not safe to be on the floor of a moving vehicle."

I smirk at him and unzip his pants.

"But it is fun! I am sure I am safe with you here. Besides, this is me thanking my knight in shining armor for earlier. Your dick will be safe between my lips."

I remove his dick from his pants; it's engorged and wet ready for my waiting lips.

"Goddess, I love you. No thanks is necessary."

His heart is beating fast.

I do what I want; what I want is to make Spence burst!

I kiss the tip.

Lick from base to tip.

He is already squirming; I love a responsive man!

I lick up and down once again, caressing his dick with my tongue.

"Fuck, baby!"

That's right, get loud!

I love to hear how my man likes what I am doing.

I take him fully down my throat. It's a good thing I don't have a gag reflex.

I suck and lick faster and faster the louder he gets.

"Fuck!"

Yes!

"TORE!"

More!

"YES!"

YES!!

"Faster, Baby! Don't stop! I am so fucking close!"

YES!

You don't have to tell me twice!

I suck and lick faster and harder; I speed up even more as I feel him convulsing.

"YES! RIGHT THERE! FUUUUUUCK!"

He climaxes in my mouth; he tastes like kettle corn.

It's an odd flavor for cum, but so sweet and satisfying.

I climb onto his lap and wrap my arms around his neck.

"How was that, Spence?"

He grabs my face roughly and kisses me!

No man has ever kissed me after a blow job; I like this.

He looks lovingly into my eyes, "Perfect, just like you, my Goddess."

Oh yeah, I can get used to being loved and appreciated like this.

I do feel like their Goddess.

Chapter 52

Gabriel

Y ou have got to be fucking kidding me?!

How dare Spencer lay his hands on me?

Does he truly understand who I am and what I stand for?

Tori was mine long before she ever became his; for him to assert his claim over her in such a brazen manner is not just audacious—it's outright unacceptable!

But now, my focus is no longer fixed on winning Tori back.

No, my thoughts have shifted to a much darker path; they will all pay for this betrayal, one way or another.

The consequences of their actions will not go unpunished.

I don't care who I kill, but at least one of the three will die.

Tori will beg me, and that will be the last thing she does.

Chapter 53

Connor

"You have got to be shitting me! He put his fucking hands on you again! Does he not understand that we can kill him?"

Tori and Spencer are nestled comfortably on either side of me on our cozy couch, situated in the welcoming warmth of Tori's house.

Tori's charming abode boasts three spacious bedrooms and spans an impressive 2,000 square feet, filled with light and character.

The inviting atmosphere wraps around us as we share moments, a perfect setting for anything we face.

Tori has no idea that I've secretly taken over her mortgage payments, a gesture I hope will express my gratitude for welcoming me back into her life.

With each payment, I'm reminded of the weight lifted off her shoulders and the chance to help her find peace in her home again.

It's my way of showing her how much I appreciate her forgiveness and the opportunity for a fresh start together.

"Spence handled it perfectly, and I lost my cool because I felt like he was trying to force me back to him. I may have gotten a little carried away and smacked him, but he pushed my buttons. But Spence was a little rough with him, and it was so hot! Which is why Spence and I had a tiny sexual moment in the car."

I chuckle, "Goddess, you have your freedom as both a couple and individually; there's nothing to be ashamed of! But we do need to figure out how to handle him properly. He thinks he can get away with anything. Who does he think he is?"

"He's your brother, Connor. That's what the background check came back with. I am so sorry, Chance. But handle my hand and let me get all I have found out."

I kiss Spence's cheek, "Go ahead, baby. I am a big boy."

Tore and Spence grip both of my hands.

"He was born two years after you. Cornelis is on his birth certificate. Turns out his mother was your dad's mistress until two years ago. She died two years ago from suffocation. Your dad didn't kill her; Gabriel killed her. He killed her because he tried to sue your dad. Gabriel and Cornelis have been working together for years to rape and belittle over one hundred women. He took his mother's last name so no one would make the connection. Cornelis's bank records reveal a pattern of financial generosity, as they illustrate that he had been depositing thousands of dollars into Gabriel's account each month for several years. These transactions, often amounting to five or even six-figure sums, appear to have started shortly after Gabriel took the significant leap, suggesting a long-standing arrangement or a deep-seated trust between the two. So, Connor, we need to end him just like we did his dad."

"Pause! You two killed Cornelis? Are you two contract killers now?"

Poor, sweet, and innocent Tore.

Connor nods at me so I can tell her.

"Yes, Goddess. We killed him for you. He ordered the hit on your parents even after I left; we were able to confirm it. He was also raping women and laundering money. He deserved every bit of what we did to him."

Tore lays her head on my shoulder and reaches to grab Spence's hand.

"Thank you both. But do you really have proof that Gabe has raped women?"

Spence sighs, "Yes, Goddess. I do, but I will not show it to you. We know you had an intimate relationship with him, so we want you involved in the least way possible. You are still too pure to see the images I saw; he is almost more vicious than his father. Don't worry, your precious head, Goddess. We will take care of him and enjoy every second of it. He deserves to die for his crimes."

Damn right, he does!

He needs to suffer more than his father did.

"Chance, are you okay? I know this is a lot of information to drop on you all at once."

His concern is incredibly sweet, and I can feel warmth spreading through me at his words.

What I love even more is that he affectionately calls me 'Chance.'

It feels personal and intimate.

At that moment, I realized how meaningful this gesture was—it told me that his affection for me was just as strong as his love for Tore.

It's a comforting thought, knowing that I hold a special place in his heart.

"I am okay. It was not the way I wanted to find out I had a sibling, but we would handle it. He will suffer more so than his dear old dad did. Not only did he touch and try to coerce someone we love, but he has been raping and degrading women for a long time. He will never harm another soul. He will never get the chance to even look in your direction again, Goddess."

He will beg for mercy, and he will get none!

Chapter 54

Gabriel

Two weeks later…

I have been laying low, carefully evading capture; her fierce guard dogs have proven ineffective at tracking my movements.

Rumor is they've been searching for me around the clock, but I've managed to outsmart them at every turn.

To ensure my safety, I enlisted one of my trusted female companions to secure a spacious warehouse two blocks from Kastaways, a popular spot in the area.

The warehouse is vast and eerily empty, with thick walls that muffle sound, making it the perfect hideout.

I've also deployed several drones to monitor Tori and the comings and goings at Kastaways.

In this coastal town, drones are a common sight, blending seamlessly into the environment, so no one has raised any suspicions about my surveillance efforts.

I know her routine now and the guard dog routine, too.

Tori will head out for lunch at two pm; the club is open today at noon.

It's Monday, so the club opens early and closes late.

On Mondays, she always goes out for lunch so she can video chat with Kass, but from the early morning video call, I saw that as Tori was arriving at the club, Kass canceled.

But know Tori, she is a creature of habit.

My plan will play out perfectly!

She eats lunch at the cafe next to the warehouse; one of my companions will lure her out.

Then I will lock her in this warehouse and have fun with her!

She better hope her guard dogs find her because I'll be the last thing she sees if they don't.

I am prepared for whatever may happen; I have guns, knives, rope, scissors, and even tape.

She will not escape my grasp!

She will be mine, or she will die!

Chapter 55

Spencer

"**W**here the hell is he, baby?"

Connor's fingers glide gently through my hair as I immerse myself in my research about Gabriel's whereabouts.

He persuaded me to abandon my usual distractions and come to the house, where I now sit in the spacious office, surrounded by the quiet hum of productivity.

Perched on the arm of my grand throne chair, Connor embodies a sense of calm.

He believes that our physical connection enhances his thinking, and as I lean into his touch, I can't help but feel that he might be right.

"He's likely gone underground, opting for a low-profile existence to avoid any unwanted attention. Shannon mentioned that ever since the day he was abruptly fired, she hadn't received a single message from him. In a surprising twist of fate, she stumbled upon the fact that he had inadvertently left his phone behind at the club that night and never returned to retrieve it. Fortunately, Shannon managed to gain access to his device, where she found a trove of crucial data. I quickly forwarded all the information from his phone to Corey, who is Massimo's trusted IT specialist and a whiz with tech. Corey confidently assured me that he would meticulously analyze the data and promised to have a detailed report ready for us later today."

As I stood deep in thought, Connor leaned in and pressed a gentle kiss on my cheek, his eyes filled with concern. "What should we do, baby? Should we ramp up Tore's security measures? What's the plan? He can't have her; she's our Goddess," he said, his voice steady yet laced with tension.

It's incredibly sweet that he's always so protective of us; his heart is genuinely huge, brimming with love and loyalty.

Never did I imagine that I would fall for a kind-hearted younger man like Connor, whose unwavering support makes me feel cherished and empowered.

"Let's wait and see what Corey comes back with. Tore is pretty guarded at the club, so we don't have much to worry about. We will find Gabriel, and once this is all over, the three of us can take a big vacation together. We will be able to decompress together and just spend time loving each other."

Connor gently tilts my head towards him, his deep, warm gaze locking onto mine. "Sounds like a dream," he murmurs, his voice a soft, inviting whisper that sends a shiver down my spine.

His lips, full and inviting, pull me in with an undeniable allure.

Each brush against my skin feels electrifying, igniting a warmth within me that chases away my worries and fears.

The sweetness of his kiss envelops me like a soft blanket, and the delicate texture of his lips against mine feels like a tender caress, calming my racing heart.

I could remain in this blissful state indefinitely, enveloped in his warm embrace, feeling the profound safety of his love surrounding me like a soft cocoon.

Yet, my unease lingers at the edges of this tranquility, ready to vanish the moment we receive word that our Goddess is safe.

I'm reluctant to part my lips from his; they feel like a comforting security blanket, shielding me from the chaos outside.

But then, the sharp, jarring ring of his phone pierces through our intimate bubble, shattering the magical spell that had enveloped us.

He shows me the screen.

Shannon never calls him.

He answers and puts it on speaker.

"Hey Shan. What's up?"

There is a definite panic in her voice, "Sir, you need to come down to Kastaways. Tori hasn't returned from lunch. A purple rose was taped to the back door with a note that reads, 'Violet is going to have some violent days. Woof, woof! Time is ticking.' I am scared sir, what is happening?"

Connor looks at me, worried, completely etching his features.

But he collects himself to help calm Shannon, "Shan, me, and Spence are on our way. Don't panic; just shut the club down. We will tell you everything when we get there. We have everything under control."

"Yes, sir. I am on it!"

Connor ends the call and punches the wall.

"FUCK!"

My heart races, the rhythm pounding in my chest like a drum, each beat resonating with a mounting sense of anger and an overwhelming wave of panic.

I feel the heat rise in my cheeks, and my palms grow clammy as thoughts begin to spiral out of control, tightening their grip around my throat like an unyielding vise.

The world around me blurs, and I struggle to focus, grappling with the chaotic emotions swirling within me.

I take a deep breath, "Let's get to the club and see what we can find before we jump to crazy conclusions. We know who did t, buthis now we just have to find her and end him."

I gently wrap my arms around Connor, pulling him close, and plant a tender kiss on his forehead, feeling the warmth of his skin beneath my lips.

A wave of unease washes over me, a nagging sense that something ominous is on the horizon.

Chapter 56

O<small>W</small>!

What's causing this throbbing pain in my head and the sharp twinge in my ribs?

Where am I, exactly?

Why does the air around me carry the smell of stagnation, like an old, forgotten room?

Why am I unable to move my hands or legs?

And why is everything enveloped in darkness—why can't I see?

Gather your thoughts, Tore!

What's the last memory that flickers in the depths of my mind?

I remember sitting at the café, savoring my lunch, soaking up the ambiance, and preparing to head back to Kastaways.

Then, I met a young girl, perhaps no older than twenty, who appeared distressed.

She asked for my help in finding her purse, claiming she had been robbed near the warehouse.

Despite my hesitation, I agreed to accompany her there to investigate.

We didn't find it, but someone hit me from behind in the head with what felt like a baseball bat.

Then, to make sure I was down, they hit me in the ribs with it; that's the last thing I remember.

Who the heck is doing this?

I hear footsteps.

Then, a rough hand strokes my cheek.

I hear something metal echo off the wooden chair I am restrained to.

Fuck!

It's a knife.

Whoever is here is dragging it across my skin.

My breath hitches, "Please, don't hurt me! I don't know why I am here, but if you tell me what you want, I will give it to you!"

I hear a modulated laugh that echoes with an unsettling resonance, and then they speak in a voice that is unsettlingly deep and robotic, each word dripping with an artificial chill.

"I have what I want. You will do everything I say; if you do, I won't hurt you too badly. But you will not leave here until I have had my fun and my revenge!"

I feel the tears running down my face.

I just got back into the right headspace; I was loving life.

I don't want to die!

The blackness will not come back!

I will not die!

I will fight!

I have worked too damn hard to die now!

I will taunt them; I will not make this easy on them!

"You think you are big and bad; you want to mask your voice, so I don't know who you are. That's a pussy move. I have gone through so much shit in my life that I am not afraid of a pussy in a mask! You want to kill me? Do it! I have tried to kill myself before. I am grateful I didn't succeed. I am not scared of dying or living. What I am scared of is not being loved. What I am scared of is not leaving a legacy behind! I don't know who the hell you are, and I don't care! You picked the wrong woman to mess with! Tell Mr. Masked Pussy, do you know what the Bratva is?"

They cough behind the mask, "Of course I do! But they have nothing to do with this or you!"

"Oh, bless your heart! That's where you are wrong, honey! Lift my sleeve; you will find my tattoo with the roman numeral three underneath it. I am third in command of women's regimen. I may look all sweet and innocent, but I gave my life to them. So, you better be prepared to face whatever you do to me!"

Now, I regret wearing my favorite long-sleeved purple shirt.

They skim the knife down my arm, slitting my sleeve all the way to my right wrist.

"Fuck! I knew there was something suspicious about you! I should have known by the weird shit Kassani said at the ceremony."

Ding, ding, ding!

They were at the reopening!

That narrows it down, but who is it?

Guy or girl?

"Fuck it! I am already in too deep! You are going to die by my hand; I don't care what those Bratva goons do to me."

Next thing I know, the knife is against my neck, and then it slides down my chest, cutting my favorite shirt to bits.

The modulated voice is next to my ear, "I will have my fun and my revenge. I hope your big ass missed me, Sugar."

You have got to be kidding me!

Only one asshole calls me that.

"Take my blindfold off, you asshole! I know who you are! Let me go so I can kill you myself!"

"Not yet, Sugar! I will get what I want, so I won't let you go. But I will give you the gift of sight."

He nestles comfortably in my lap, his weight barely a whisper against my thighs.

I understand his intentions; he desires to assert his little kingdom, demonstrating that he holds the reins in this intimate but non-consensual moment.

He probably gets off on watching me squirm.

He knows me too well; he knows I like closeness.

But this repulses me; only my men get these intimate moments.

He finally removes the blindfold.

My eyes take a moment to adjust.

Holy shit!

I am so uncomfortable right now; he sits across my lap, shirtless in nothing but a pair of boxers.

He slowly removes the modulator mask that covers his whole face.

He licks my cheek and whispers, "Did you miss me, Sugar?"

I swiftly turn my head to the side.

"NO, YOU ASSHOLE! GET OFF ME, GABE!"

"Scream all you want, Sugar. This place is soundproof; I have big plans for you! I will show you what it's like to be with a real man, and I will teach you to beg and obey! When I am done with you, no man will want you, or you will be dead. That will all depend on how willing you are."

"FUCK YOU! BLACK! BLACK! BLACK!"

That was the last thing I was able to say before the syringe slid into my neck.

Chapter 57

Gabriel

I didn't want to have to drug her; her screaming was on my nerves!

I will make her suffer when she wakes up.

I didn't know she was part of the Bratva!

I thought she was just one of Connor's whores.

Shit!

There's is no way I will make it out of this alive.

Soon, Connor will find out we are related, but I doubt that will stop him from coming after me.

I have done too many bad things for him to let me go.

I now believe he and Spencer killed my father.

The last time my contact heard from him was right before he came to meet Spencer down here.

But that doesn't matter right now; I will get my revenge on my father and for them turning Tori against me!

She may be too fat for me, but that was the decision for me.

Not for two men to take her from me!

As soon as she wakes up, I will teach her how to beg!

Poor Tori, it looks like your guard dogs are not coming to save you.

Chapter 58

Kass

My phone is freaking out, it is blaring an alarm.

OH SHIT!

That is my Tori alarm!

I had her necklace programmed so that if she says black three times, it would send me her location.

I pull up my safety app.

Why is she at the abandoned warehouse?

It's a good thing I flew in this morning; that's why I called Tore this morning.

I was coming to visit just to check on things since Spencer contacted Corey.

Let me head into Kastaways and get some backup before I storm the warehouse.

Spencer's car is sitting outside. Hopefully, Connor is here too.

As I enter with my key, I see them hunched over the bar, looking like they are trying to form a plan.

"You better tell me what you two are doing and why I got an SOS from Tori!"

They both look startled, "My Queen! Why are you here? What SOS?"

Spencer has always been formal with me, just like Dorian.

"I programmed Tori's necklace to send me her location if she says the word black three times. Tori knew I was coming today. I wanted to check on things, and I brought the data that Corey found he just sent to me. So again, tell me what the hell is going on so we can go save Tori! She is right down the road, so talk fast! If she dies, I will kill you both!"

They tell me everything.

If they don't kill the little fucker I will!

"She's at the abandoned warehouse two blocks away. Let's go! He will die today! Connor alert the clean-up crew."

Chapter 59

Gabriel

She's finally starting to stir; I untied her from the chair while she was asleep.

But only long enough to retie her hands and feet that way, she can beg me.

She will either suck my dick, or I will slit her throat.

Her eyes flutter open, grab the back of her head and tug.

She is startled; she takes in my fully naked body, and that's when the fear sets in.

"Did you have a nice nap, Sugar? I am so glad you did! Time for your lesson, suck my dick or die."

She spits to the side.

"You want my whorish lips on your dick? I wouldn't if I were you. Not only because you don't know who my lips have been on but also because Hailey taught me how to bite a dick off. So, your choice, Sugar!"

I wince at the thought of losing my manhood.

I let go of her hair and let her drop to the floor.

I go grab my jeans and slide them back on and don my holster just in case; you can never be too careful around the Bratva whores.

I sigh, "Listen, I have to get some things off my chest before I kill you, Sugar. Is that okay?"

"Be my guest; it's not like I am going anywhere."

Chapter 60

A heavy sense of dread settles over me once again.

Please, let Tori be alive!

Kass and Connor are heading toward the front, their silhouettes barely visible against the dim light. I'm slipping around to the back, heart pounding in my chest.

As I creep closer to the back door, I can hear Gabriel's voice drifting through the shadows, each word laced with malice.

"Before I kill you, you must know how I really feel about you, Sugar. Honestly, you are not my type; you're too fat for me. I never loved you. My entire plan was to treat you like I did all the other women, make them fall in love with me, and then milk them for all they are worth! A woman's place is only in the kitchen and bed, pleasing her man in every way. But I am repulsed by your size; I prefer my women size six or smaller, not size whale."

What an asshole!

Tore knows how beautiful she is, and Connor and I make sure she never forgets that.

I hear Tore laugh, "Yeah, keep telling yourself that, buddy! I was there too, remember? Your teenie weenie was not repulsed by me. I had you come in minutes, but I only came if I got off after our three-minute encounter! You're not hurting me, Sugar! I know how beautiful I am, and I have two men who remind me every day. Two men who know how to make me squirt and come within minutes! Two men who love me and don't have shrimp dicks like you. Spence's big toe is bigger than your dick, hell Spence's dick is bigger than your bicep and Connor's too!"

Way to go, baby!

I love this woman; she's all fight!

She is not taking his insults lying down!

"Shut up! You whore!"

Tore chuckles, "Pick a new insult, Sugar. I am not a whore just because I love two men. Oh, I see. You're jealous, Sugar!"

Oh shit!
Time to bust in!

Gabe just cocked his gun!

Fuck!

I unholster my gun and take off sprinting.

"Jealous? Are you jealous that this bullet is still in my gun and not in you? Don't worry, Sugar. It's about to enter you; I hope you squirt!"

I dive and shoot, did I miss?

BANG!

BANG!

Why do my eyes feel so heavy?

Chapter 61

Tori

This is it.

This is how I die.

Spencer, I love you and our new love.

Connor, I love you and our new but old love.

Please watch over Shannon Kass and Kastaways.

I open my tear-filled eyes as two shots sound.

The next thing I knew, Spence was diving in front of me!

"NO! SPENCE! MOVE!"

The bullet pierces his chest, and he falls to the ground; I scoot as fast as I can to him.

Here comes the full waterworks; I can't hold it back.

My hands and feet are still tied; I kiss his cheek to get his attention.

"Spence, no! Why? Why, baby?"

He smirks sadly at me, "I told you I would do anything for you. Promise me something, Goddess."

I can barely see through all the tears.

"Anything, baby! Anything for you, Spence!"

His bloody hand caresses my face, "Don't mourn me long, but most of all, marry Connor. Get your second chance; be torn no more. I love you, Goddess. Take care of yourself and our Chance. Don't ever go back to the blackness. I love you, and tell Connor I love him, too."

My selfless, Spence.

"Anything for you, my baby. I love you, forever and always."

"Make the last thing I remember your lips, Goddess."

Anything for Spence.

I bend down the best I can and kiss his lips.

I put all my love, passion, and soul into that kiss.

I slowly sit up, and as I do, I see it.

The light leaves Spence's eyes.

"NO! NO! SPENCE COMEBACK! NO! NO! BLACK! BLACK! BLACK!"

The last thing I see before I pass out is a figure that looks like Kass running towards me.

My sweet…

Chapter 62

Epilogue- Connor

Three Months Later…

Today, Tore and I have been married for one and a half months.
Tore and I mourned Spence as long as he would have allowed.

Exactly one and a half months, it still hurts.

But we are getting threw it together.

Today, we are going to Spence's grave to tell him our news.

As we arrive at the graveyard, the sadness returns to Tore's eyes.

We walk through the gravestones until we find the most important one.

His headstone reads:

Spencer Peck
Beloved For all Eternity.

I put my arm around Tore, "Tell him, Goddess. You know he is always listening."

She nods, "Hi, Spence. I love and miss you. Today, we found out that we are pregnant. We are only six weeks along, but we wanted to tell you. If it's a boy, his name will be Spence. We will never forget you; we wish you were here to do this with us."

Tore looks up at me and snuggles into my chest, the tears falling now.

We will love you forever and always, Spence.

Thank you for showing us what we needed.

Thank you for giving us our second chance.

Rest easy, Spence.

Chapter 63

I ran from my previous life as a punching bag.

I was married for five years.

To a man who used me as his own personal punching bag.

Then, on the day Kass killed Tara Ashley, my life changed forever.

Shannon Warren was born and put under Bratva protection.

It's been four years; I should be safe.

Right?

Should I fall in love or be married to my job?

THE END….. FOR NOW

Thank you for reading Summer N Dawn's work!
Summer is a small-town girl with cerebral palsy who never lets life get her down.
She loves to create worlds where everyone is welcome to be free and fun!
Always remember, stay dark and spread the love!